She felt i
he sensed a latent strength.

He had a feeling he shouldn't underestimate her. After all, she'd managed to ditch her bodyguards and avoid her brother.

He looked down at her and she lifted her face. She smiled. It made something inside Ares ache. Why was she so smiley? So perky? She was a princess way out of her depth. She could have been unconscious somewhere now if it hadn't been for him. But again he had that sense that perhaps she would have surprised him by managing to get out of that predicament. She was using a false name to avoid detection.

Then his gaze went to her mouth. It opened slightly and he had a glimpse of a pink tongue. White teeth. A fire started raging in his blood. He'd never been more tempted by a woman. By a woman who was so far out of his bounds that—

Before Ares could formulate another word, she'd reached up and pressed her mouth to his, a chaste and surprisingly sweet gesture. But any thought of *sweet* fast dissolved as *sweet* morphed into burning hot *heat* and intense need. Ares couldn't resist.

*A spectacular new royal duet
from Harlequin Presents author Abby Green!*

Royal House of Sadat

A crown in crisis...

Royal scandal has rocked the unshakable house of Sadat. When news of the late king's affair shocks the nation, his heir, King Caius, is forced to abdicate. Now his sister, Princess Cassie, must take up the mantle.

Their futures were once etched in stone. But with the line of succession altered forever, can Sadat's royal siblings take destiny into their own hands?

Find out in

Bodyguard's Royal Temptation

Desperate for one final taste of freedom before her coronation, Crown Princess Cassie escapes to the shimmering shores of Greece. Her brother's best friend, Ares, security tycoon and now her personal bodyguard, isn't far behind her! She might resent his presence, but can't deny the irresistible magnetism between them...

Available now!

And look out for

Caius and Poppy's story

Former King Caius is embracing life as a playboy tycoon. Until a red-hot rendezvous with a masked stranger in Paris has royal consequences that threaten his newfound bachelor status! If the shock of first fatherhood wasn't enough, he discovers his anonymous beauty is his once betrothed, Crown Princess Poppy of Valdere!

Coming soon!

BODYGUARD'S ROYAL TEMPTATION

ABBY GREEN

PRESENTS

If you purchased this book without a cover you should be aware that this book is stolen property. It was reported as "unsold and destroyed" to the publisher, and neither the author nor the publisher has received any payment for this "stripped book."

Recycling programs for this product may not exist in your area.

ISBN-13: 978-1-335-21370-9

Bodyguard's Royal Temptation

Copyright © 2026 by Abby Green

All rights reserved. No part of this book may be used or reproduced in any manner whatsoever without written permission.

Without limiting the exclusive rights of any author, contributor or the publisher of this publication, any unauthorized use of this publication to train generative artificial intelligence (AI) technologies is expressly prohibited. Harlequin also exercises their rights under Article 4(3) of the Digital Single Market Directive 2019/790 and expressly reserves this publication from the text and data mining exception.

This is a work of fiction. Names, characters, places and incidents are either the product of the author's imagination or are used fictitiously. Any resemblance to actual persons, living or dead, businesses, companies, events or locales is entirely coincidental.

For questions and comments about the quality of this book, please contact us at CustomerService@Harlequin.com.

TM and ® are trademarks of Harlequin Enterprises ULC.

 Harlequin Enterprises ULC
22 Adelaide St. West, 41st Floor
Toronto, Ontario M5H 4E3, Canada
www.Harlequin.com

HarperCollins Publishers
Macken House, 39/40 Mayor Street Upper,
Dublin 1, D01 C9W8, Ireland
www.HarperCollins.com

Printed in Lithuania

Irish author **Abby Green** ended a very glamorous career in film and TV—which really consisted of a lot of standing in the rain outside actors' trailers—to pursue her love of romance. After she'd bombarded Harlequin with manuscripts, they kindly accepted one, and an author was born. She lives in Dublin, Ireland, and loves any excuse for distraction. Visit abby-green.com or email abbygreenauthor@gmail.com.

Books by Abby Green

Harlequin Presents

His Housekeeper's Twin Baby Confession
Heir for His Empire
"I Do" for Revenge
Rush to the Altar
Billion-Dollar Baby Shock
Bride of Betrayal

Princess Brides for Royal Brothers

Mistaken as His Royal Bride

Hot Winter Escapes

Claimed by the Crown Prince

Brazilian Billionaire Brothers

The Heir Dilemma
On His Bride's Terms

Visit the Author Profile page
at Harlequin.com for more titles.

This is for Paddy Kerr—thanks for the invaluable sailing/boats advice. And this is also for the rest of the Brookfield Walkies group, Jo and Anita.
Not to mention the dogs: Gunner, Poppy, Juno, Orwell and Peggy. Thanks for the many steps and things put to rights on our little treks around IMMA. The perfect recipe for staying sane(ish). x

CHAPTER ONE

THE VOICE DRONED ON... 'Given our location between North Africa and Southern Europe, and the fact that we are steeped in history dating back thousands of years, with influences from the Moors to the Greeks, Spanish and French, we are uniquely positioned to—'

'To promote our rich diverse culture and stunning natural beauty by encouraging investment in industry and especially tourism. Having French as our official language and with most citizens speaking English and at least two or three more, we're accessible to many, in terms not only of tourism but also industry. We need to encourage our young, well-educated and multilingual population to stay, and not emigrate as so many have in the past, but to do that we need to prove we can provide investment opportunities.'

Her Royal Highness, Crown Princess Cassandra Theodora Sophia Beatriz Clotilde Mansur de Roche—to give her her full name and title—finished off the end of her chief advisor's lecture without even thinking about it. Anything to stay awake. His voice was so unfortunately monotonous. Her older brother, the recently abdicated king, had warned her about this.

She was also standing in front of open French doors that led out to a terrace, in a bid to remain alert with the help of the sea breeze. The view of aforementioned stunning scenery beyond the palace offices was helping. The blue ocean glittered and foamed under the sparkling sun, she could see a pod of dolphins frolicking and wished she were out there too, in her little kayak, exploring the nooks and crannies of the coast. The dolphins would regularly keep her company.

But that had been when she'd been the mere spare to the heir. Just a plain princess. Before the world had blown up a couple of months ago when it had transpired that her older brother was *not* the biological heir of the late king. He was in fact the product of an affair their late mother, the queen, had had with a lover. Probably one of her bodyguards.

Cassie had always wondered if the whispered rumours were true because the only physical trait she and her brother shared was their distinctive blue eyes. Where she was blonde, and fair, he was dark. Well, now she knew. Now everyone knew.

Everything had changed and suddenly Cassie had been pushed to the top of the heir queue. The coveted spot. A part of her was still in denial, although these daily lectures covering everything from history to geography, economics and politics were helping to drum it home.

In a few short weeks, she would be crowned Queen of Sadat Sur Mer. At that reminder there came a familiar tightening in her chest and her breathing became shallower. She'd worked hard to overcome the anxiety that had dogged her childhood dominated by two parents who'd hated each other and who had expressed that frequently and volubly within the palace walls. She'd battled it by focusing on being as sunny and amenable as possible, in a bid to distract one or other of her parents from hating on each other at any given time.

She'd been so successful at projecting a happy-go-lucky front that she'd managed to almost fool herself into believing it was her default disposition. And it had worked most of the time—her bright beaming smile would often help divert attention from her parents' rigid tension and barely concealed contempt for one another.

So the return of the old anxiety was not welcome. Nor was the fact that her brother was no longer here to guide her or to help her with this transition. Not his fault—but the backlash against him for not being of the king's line had been fierce. The people had loved Caius and had felt personally betrayed by something that had been entirely out of his control.

It had been decided that he would serve Cassie better by leaving Sadat Sur Mer until her coronation day, to let things calm down and give the people time to adjust to her taking on the role of monarch.

Cassie knew Caius would be with her if he could but she couldn't help but also feel a little irrationally betrayed by the fact that now she was all on her own to deal with this massive change in their situation. She'd always been able to count on his solid and comforting presence, even if he'd been on the other side of the world, making headlines for his playboy antics before he'd been crowned king. He'd barely had enough time to settle into the role before the scandal of his birth had hit them.

It wasn't that she didn't want to be queen, she'd just never expected to be in this position. He'd been brought up prepared to be ruler. She hadn't. And now everyone was looking to her to be their supreme leader. Daunting, to say the least.

A pang of old grief struck her to think of her twin sister, Christabel, who had died at birth. If she had lived, who was to say that Cassie would have even become queen? Maybe her sister would have relished the role and been more suited? But she wasn't here, and Cassie was, and that was a humbling reminder that she had to accept this new reality for her sister's sake as much as hers.

'Your Highness?'

Cassie reluctantly turned from the view to see folders open on the desk. 'Yes, Pierre.'

'One more item to discuss before we finish.'

She could make out the A4-size photo of a blandly handsome face from where she stood. Clearly they'd moved on from her chief advisor's favourite subject to his next favourite subject—a prospective mate. The king to her queen. The sire to her heirs, who would carry her name to ensure the line didn't disappear. The band around her chest got tighter and she countered it by forcing a bright smile as she walked over to the desk and sat down behind it.

'You've prepared some candidates, I see.'

'Yes, Your Highness. The men in this folder are all from eminently suitable royal lineages. As you might appreciate considering recent events, it's absolutely crucial that we restore faith in our people by choosing someone with impeccable pedigree.'

With superb comic timing, Cassie's beloved cockapoo, whose pedigree was murky to say the least, ambled over from her bed to where Cassie sat, and Cassie scooped her into her lap, ignoring Pierre's pinched expression of disapproval. She didn't appreciate the reference to her brother being somehow *less* just because his royal blood was a little diluted.

She sent Pierre a tight smile. 'Thank you, I can look through these on my own.'

Her advisor all but clicked his heels together and bowed. 'Very well, Your Highness, we can make arrangements to meet your preferred candidates.'

Cassie hid a sigh and said, 'Pierre, you really don't have to bow to me. I would prefer to keep things a little less formal than they have been.' Especially as they'd been in her father's time. A father who had shown scant interest in Cassie, or only when she'd diverted his attention by being sweet and pretty and happy.

Pierre looked as scandalised as if she'd started to strip off her clothes.

'Your Highness, there is a long tradition of protocol to follow. It is my duty to ensure this is preserved, now more than ever given our recent tribulations.'

Cassie swallowed her frustration. It would take time to shake things up a bit. She knew that. 'Pierre, as always I appreciate all your counsel and hard work.'

Looking slightly mollified, the older man left and when he had Cassie slumped back into the chair, snuggling Zoe close. Caius, her brother, had warned her that the old guard would be hard to encourage into modern times.

She sat up again and looked at the open folder. The first candidate was someone she was distantly related to. *Euw.* No. She flicked to the next candidate. A prince known for his love of illegal substances. A hard no. The next one had gambled away his family's fortune and was known to be on the lookout for a new monarchy to feather his nest. No. The last one in the folder was gay—an open secret. *No.*

Cassie shut the folder and tried not to feel disheartened. If she truly felt one of them might be a possibility as her life partner then she would do her best to give them a chance. She didn't want to be obstructive.

Even Caius, who'd partied as hard as the rest of them while he was crown prince, before ascending to the throne, had agreed to discuss forming an engagement with a crown princess from one of Europe's most illustrious bloodlines and monarchies. That arrangement had dissolved once the scandal had hit.

But before that had happened, when Cassie had asked her brother how he could endure the thought of a marriage of convenience he'd shrugged and said, 'This is our world, Cass. We don't have the luxury of choosing our own partner. And in any case, it's better like this, we both know there's no such thing as love or happy ever afters.'

Cassie hadn't responded to that because her dirty

little secret was that she did want to believe in love and happy ever after. Especially after enduring a childhood watching two people slowly and torturously annihilate each other, spreading toxicity and infecting everything around them with cynicism.

A cynicism that her brother had embraced, telling Cassie all he needed out of a marriage was an heir and maybe a spare and no drama or histrionics.

She wasn't even sure when this burning desire had rooted itself within her. Maybe it had its genesis in knowing she had got to live and her sister hadn't, so she wanted a more authentic experience.

But once it had become apparent that she would become queen, she knew she couldn't embark on that life of service with someone by her side that she only tolerated. And none of the men in that folder came even close to being tolerated, never mind a potential *real* partner.

She wasn't naive enough to expect actual *love*, but was it too much to hope for respect? Companionship, kindness. Even passion? Although that was still an abstract concept. No one had ever stirred her desires like that. She was still a virgin. Not from lack of opportunity—she'd gone to the local university and had friends of both sexes but, as a princess, it wasn't exactly easy to indulge in a relationship when every public move you made was studied and scrutinised. When you had your own security detail.

Her brother had cautioned her before he'd left Sadat Sur Mer, saying, 'Cass, I know you've got a soft heart but you need to be strategic about who you choose. If you can find someone who will let you rule and be by your side and give you heirs, that's all you need. You can find passion and excitement elsewhere if you're discreet about it. This is a job.'

'Is that what you'd planned to do?' Cassie had asked her brother, feeling almost doubly betrayed by his blatant cynicism.

He'd shrugged. 'Sure, and I wouldn't have judged my queen for doing the same, as long as we were both discreet.'

But that hadn't worked for their parents. Their respective infidelities hadn't eased matters, they'd caused bitter tension. Cassie had always secretly suspected that her father had been in love with their beautiful mother, and he hadn't been able to tolerate her affairs, or the fact that she didn't love him.

Cassie sighed out loud in the massive and ornate palace private office. All the more reason for her *not* to pursue finding a real relationship. Maybe her brother was right.

But then something rebellious sparked to life within her as she realised that perhaps embarking on a life of duty would be a lot more palatable if she felt she'd *lived* a little first.

Maybe that was why Caius had been so sanguine about a life of service with someone he would never love. Because he'd had his fun as one of the world's most notorious playboys and he'd felt ready to settle down to a more sedate and discreet life. Cassie stood up abruptly and put the dog down.

She started to pace back and forth as a plan formed

in her head. An audacious plan. She'd never rebelled in her life, too busy trying to make sure everyone around her was happy. She'd never joined the club of Euro royalty who indulged in an endless merry-go-round of exclusive parties, shopping and sybaritic opulent experiences.

She stopped pacing as it struck her that the reason she hadn't ever indulged like that was because it didn't really appeal. She was more introverted. She liked reading. She loved clothes and fashion but for her own pleasure, not to show off in public. She'd never been able to indulge in the side of her that veered towards bright colours and floaty ethereal dresses more suited to a free spirit than a princess.

She'd always wondered if maybe her sister would have been the more extroverted one.

But maybe she could find out what that freedom would be like. Just for a brief moment, before the world as she knew it turned into something else. A life of duty and service. Surely if she felt as if she'd taken something for herself, this desire for a more fulfilling personal life wouldn't have such an appeal.

She just needed to live a little. To take a leaf out of her brother's book and enjoy her freedom before it was gone for good. *Maybe even lose her virginity.* Her skin felt hot at that audacious idea, but it also took root. She had no desire to offer herself up to her prospective king as some kind of sacrificial virgin.

The days of expecting such archaic things were long gone and she knew well that not one of those prospective kings in the folder was a virgin. So why should she be?

But if she wanted to indulge in a last bid for freedom, she needed time, privacy and a chance to be anonymous. She knew she'd go unrecognised among throngs of people who didn't expect to see a princess in their midst. She wouldn't stand out in a crowd, if she didn't want to.

Where would she find throngs of people? In a busy tourist location.

She went back to the desk and picked up the phone, summoning Pierre back into the room.

He arrived within seconds, a hopeful look on his face, no doubt because he expected her to have chosen a suitable potential king candidate. She was going to disappoint him.

Determined not to be swayed from her course of action, she said, 'Pierre, I'm taking personal leave for the next ten days. A holiday.'

His eyes popped and his face flushed. His mouth opened but Cassie put up her hand, stopping him from saying a word. She said firmly, 'It's not up for discussion. Please rearrange my schedule.'

CHAPTER TWO

ARES DRAKOS REALLY resented having to make a last-minute dash across the globe from Manhattan to Greece. The island of Crete, specifically. He also resented, but with less force, the fact that he'd had to cancel a date with his current lover. Although if he was being totally honest with himself, he had planned on it being the last time he'd see her. She hadn't turned out to be all that interesting, in or out of bed, and he found his capacity to indulge in the games of modern dating becoming less and less appealing.

There were very few people who could call in a favour like this, because he was very selective in who he chose to protect, but Caius Mansur de Roche, recently disgraced abdicated king, was one of them. Thanks to an alcohol-infused bonding session they'd had way back in some bar in… New Orleans? Or maybe it had been Costa Rica.

Ares had been there on a job, Caius had been there raising hell. Ares—who usually loathed the rich and entitled, and royalty were the worst of that lot—had found himself actually liking the crown prince. So much so that, when he'd realised there was a paparazzo lurking, he'd tipped the crown prince off and he'd managed not to land himself on the front pages yet again.

They'd somehow always endeavoured to meet up if they were in the same place at the same time. But when Caius had abdicated and asked Ares to take over his sister's—the new crown princess's—security, Ares had refused, point-blank. He didn't do cosseted royals. He'd had a short, sharp experience with European royalty and they needed babysitters, not security. He'd vowed never again. He didn't need the money or the headache.

He used to work as a one-man security operation, highly sought after because of his legendary skills, but he now ran an exclusive security company with a very select band of employees that he trusted implicitly. They had become *the* go-to security agency in a very short space of time, not just because of their discretion and skill but because Ares had also invested in new cutting-edge decryption software, making him millions overnight but also giving him and his company an edge over everyone else. An edge he did not take advantage of, which had only garnered him even more respect.

But then Caius had contacted him again the day before and told him that his sister, Crown Princess Cassandra, had taken an unscheduled holiday break, leaving Sadat Sur Mer, the small island monarchy for Greece.

By the time she'd made it to the other side of security at the private airport in Athens, she'd somehow given her bodyguards the slip.

Ares had said, 'She's due to be crowned queen soon, right? So she's probably just making the most of her time clubbing and shopping and lounging about on yachts. I know I would.'

His friend had sounded uncharacteristically tense. 'No, Ares, she's not like that. She's quiet. She doesn't go clubbing. So, even if she is on some kind of a mission to have an…experience, she's not street smart, not like us. She's innocent, and I can't be certain about this but I do mean *literally*.'

Ares had made a face. 'That is too much information, my friend, even for you.'

But his friend had pleaded, 'Look, Ares, you know I don't scare easily. But she's only sending me texts to let me know she's OK, no more details. No information about where she is. She's out there on her own, without any protection. Our security team has let her down. Left her vulnerable. She's my baby sister. Even though it's not my fault, it *is* down to me that she's now the crown princess. I need to know she's OK and I know your team will locate her within hours if you put them on it. You know money isn't an issue.'

Ares's insides had clenched at that. He'd once had baby sisters and he could remember the way it had been totally instinctive to want to protect them. Until his family had left him for dead. He'd walked away from them as soon as he could and neither they nor his older brother had come looking for him, showing him that they hadn't ever needed him. The distance between them now seemed more vast than ever.

He'd felt himself weakening and said gruffly, 'And you know money shouldn't be discussed among friends.'

He'd taken a breath and then, 'Look, I have some meetings in Europe I've been putting off scheduling. I'll do it.' He'd felt the strangest sensation as he'd committed to that, as if he'd just committed to something momentous.

Caius had sighed volubly with relief. 'Thanks, man, I really owe you.'

Except now Ares was bitterly regretting that his friend had somehow managed to worm his way into Ares's very smallest soft spot to butter him up. Because from where he was sitting, at an incredibly tacky Cretan bar with the absolute worst affront to music pounding so loud around him that he could feel it in his bones, Crown Princess Cassandra Mansur de Roche, with a heap of middle names he couldn't care less about, was having the time of her life and looked to be in no need of rescuing or protecting at all.

He knew it was her even though her naturally blonde hair had streaks of pink, red and purple running through the long wavy locks. And even though her eyes were heavily made up and there were tiny diamanté stickers artfully placed across her cheeks. And…he couldn't be sure but from where he was sitting her eyes looked darker so maybe she was using coloured contacts, because one of her most distinctive physical traits was her incredibly blue eyes.

It irritated Ares that he could recall her picture in his mind with absolute precision. That honey-blonde hair, kissed by the sun. Wide, almond-shaped blue eyes under dark arching brows. Not too thin, not too thick. Just perfect. Like her nose, with the slightest patrician bump.

A perfectly oval-shaped face with high cheekbones. Delicate jaw, but defined. But it was her mouth that had sent little sparks of heat into his veins. Plump and full. Generous. Wide. Far too sensual a mouth for a woman who had to appear at all times to be mindful and demure.

Ares had taken one look at that mouth and had scoffed at her brother's quaint notion that she might still be an innocent. No way no how. Not with a mouth that sent all sorts of dark desires into a man's head. *Or just yours, maybe?*

He scowled at that and took another slug of beer, hoping that might douse the very unwelcome buzz of awareness in his body. He was only human and she was a beautiful woman, but blonde princesses with electric-blue eyes who looked as though they'd just stepped off a Disney movie set were not his type. The awareness was an aberration.

He assured himself again that she was not in need of specialist protection. She was dancing with total abandon in the middle of the dance floor, arms in the air, inviting the eye to move over her perfect, lissome body. Long legs encased in snug denim that cupped her perfectly shaped bottom, which Ares could see all too well as she turned away from him.

Her graceful back was bare, as she was wearing a sparkly butterfly-shaped top that seemed to be held together by two mere strings, at her neck and mid-back. Her waist was slim and her hips...surprisingly womanly. Sending another flash of heat into Ares's blood.

Dammit. He was not going to sit here and ogle a spoiled entitled princess, crown or otherwise, who clearly needed no help. He fished for his phone in the pocket of his jeans, fully intending to take a photo of Caius's precious baby sister in action to send to him before letting him know her location so her own useless bodyguard/babysitters could take over again. And then he could get on with protecting people who *really* needed to be protected, but just as he lifted the phone up, he saw something and cursed volubly. He couldn't leave her now.

Cassie knew that she must look as if she were having the time of her life and, boy, was she really trying her hardest, but the truth was that she knew she'd made a mistake coming to Crete in a bid to stay anonymous among the crowds.

It was *too* busy. And, she'd realised, she wasn't used to being in crowds without a cordon of space around her—not a bad thing, but more jarring than she had expected.

So far, her attempt at making the most of her freedom was looking a little pathetic. But the truth was that she'd really liked the idea of going to a regular holiday destination, rather than some rarefied resort.

She'd wanted to feel as though she was experiencing the real world for once.

Her close friends were people in Sadat Sur Mer who were still at university or who had jobs and families. They also weren't available to spontaneously flit away for a few days of hedonism, demonstrating the gulf between her and them that she'd always tried her best to pretend wasn't there.

Hedonism, Cassie berated herself. More like Cassie-no-matesism. Just when she was beginning to feel like a total fool for going to all the trouble to disguise herself—after realising most people here were too wasted to know who they were, never mind her—two guys about her age approached her on the dance floor, crowding her a little so she had to move back.

She was slightly assured because they looked less out of it than everyone else.

'Hey, you look lonely, want some company?' One of them leant towards Cassie and shouted in her ear over the pounding music.

He held out a glass with a bright pink liquid in it and a little umbrella cocktail stick poking out from the top. 'Try it, it's nice.'

Of course she wasn't going to accept a drink from a complete stranger. At that moment Cassie realised that, somehow, these two amenable-looking guys had manoeuvred her so that they were in a corner of the club and they were blocking her view of the dance floor. She was alone. No one knew where she was and actually this whole idea had been really stupid.

She forced a bright smile. 'Thanks, guys, but I'm

actually on my way out to meet a friend in another bar, and I'm late.'

'But you looked like you were having fun. Stay for one drink, come on.' This was said by the other guy, who had a cute friendly face. Cheeky chappie. But Cassie felt uneasy.

'I'd really like to but—'

'Then do.' The other guy, more forceful now, holding the drink towards her. Cassie's skin went cold. She felt herself tensing her muscles ready to use a couple of moves to extricate herself when a large shape loomed over them all and a hand reached into where Cassie stood and grabbed her arm.

'*There* you are. I've been waiting an hour. Come on.'

Cassie was so stunned at first that she let herself be tugged towards the stranger, barely aware of the two guys falling back. She registered things—tall, broad, powerful, dark messy hair and short beard, intense eyes, dark brows, and…the fact that the stranger was hands down the most gorgeous specimen of a man she'd ever seen in her life.

His face was hard and stern but it was also *beautiful*. His mouth in particular was captivating. Firmly sculpted. She had a strange urge to reach up and trace its shape with a finger. Cassie felt a little dazed.

Taking advantage of her surprise, his hand moved down her arm, and he took her hand to lead her out of the bar before her brain had time to catch up with her body. Simultaneously she was registering an electrical charge flowing through her blood out to her skin, making it prickle. *Awareness*.

They were outside on the busy street and Cassie's ears were still ringing from the loud music when she realised what had just happened. She pulled her hand free of the man's and looked up at him. 'What the hell do you think you're doing?'

He stood back and looked her up and down. Cassie realised he was even taller than she'd first thought. At least six feet four. Wearing a shirt with rolled-up sleeves and jeans. Jeans that sat low on narrow hips and hugged powerful thighs and long legs like a second skin.

Mortified to realise she'd just blatantly ogled him, she looked back up and folded her arms across her chest. His dark gaze dropped and Cassie looked down to see her stance was pushing her breasts together and up. The top precluded a bra and she'd been conscious that she didn't have the small tidy breasts a top like this merited but it had been too late to change earlier, before she'd lost her nerve completely and left her four-star hotel.

She refused to be conscious of him *ogling* her even though it made the awareness coalesce into a feeling of tightness deep in her core. She automatically pressed her thighs together to stem the sensation.

'Do you want to explain why you just manhandled me out of that bar?' she said, sounding unbearably prim.

He looked so stern, Cassie had a totally unexpected and disturbing image of this man putting her over his knee and lifting his hand—she blurted out in a panic, 'I was having fun.'

He arched a brow and finally deigned to speak. 'Really? It didn't look much like fun dancing on your own.' His voice matched the rest of him, deep and masculine. The slightest hint of an accent. And censure.

He was echoing her own thoughts and the fact that her decision to take this trip had been so spontaneous and last minute that she really hadn't thought it through much at all. He was also unwittingly pressing on the wound of the fact that she was alone because her brother had had to more or less abandon her.

She felt exposed and lashed back. 'Watching me, were you? Just waiting for a moment to step in and make it look like you're some sort of saviour? Well, those guys weren't bothering me at all. In fact, if you don't mind, I'm going to go back in.'

Cassie went to walk around the man mountain, because that's what he was. Powerful. With well-honed, defined muscles. Thick corded muscles. Under dark olive skin.

But before she could take another step he said, 'Wait, stop.'

Cassie wasn't sure why she did. But something about him was just too…intriguing, while also being seriously annoying. *Disturbing.*

She didn't turn around. Waiting. He moved to stand in front of her again. She looked at him and raised a brow this time. A look of definite irritation crossed with something else she couldn't decipher crossed his face. Then he gritted out as if almost loathe to give her the information, 'They had spiked that drink. Most likely with a roofie. They weren't drunk, did you notice that? They're probably on a mission to spike girls' drinks all night until they get lucky. You were pretty obviously alone so you were an easy target.'

'Can you stop saying that, please? And I'm not an easy target. I could have defended myself. I had no intention of taking that drink.' But she might have if they hadn't creeped her out. Cassie had to acknowledge that.

Mr Tall Dark and Stern pointed out, 'You wouldn't have had a hope of defending yourself if you'd taken a sip of that drink.'

Cassie shivered a little. No. She wouldn't have, and she might have let her guard down. And she had ditched her bodyguards. And the royal house of Mansur de Roche did not need adverse headlines before her coronation.

She forced herself to stand tall and say, 'OK, well, look, I appreciate you had my best interests in mind and were only trying to help.'

She held out her hand and he looked at it dumbly. She said, 'I'm offering my hand in thanks for your concern.'

As if she'd shocked him with her gesture he took it, wrapping her much smaller hand in his. She noticed his palms felt a little rough and that sent another electric jolt right to a spot between her legs. She pulled her hand back. 'OK, thanks, bye now.'

She turned to go in the opposite direction but then the man said, 'Wait. Where are you going?'

Cassie stopped and turned around again. She had to admit helplessly, 'I don't actually know. I'd like to have a drink and a dance but that place was just...*awful*.'

'There's not much better here but I know a spot if you'd like to have a drink with me.'

Cassie hovered uncertainly. Had this man been telling the truth? If she accepted his invitation was she in fact being incredibly stupid and naive and jumping from the frying pan into the fire?

She imagined if her sister were here and braver than Cassie, more spontaneous. Before she could think about it too much she acted on instinct. 'OK, yes.' She smiled and his eyes widened. He was looking at her mouth.

Then those dark eyes moved back up and with almost a scowl on his face he said, 'Come on.'

Cassie was totally bemused. This man had clearly not been born with the charm gene and yet perversely it was what made her feel safe to go with him.

He led her over to where a motorbike rested at an angle. A proper motorbike. Not a scooter as most people used here. Cassie loved motorbikes. Caius had secretly taught her how to ride them when she was much younger. The royal staff would have had collective heart attacks if they'd known. Their parents probably would have been too busy arguing to notice.

The man took a helmet out of a back compartment and handed it to her. She put it on. Then he put on his own helmet. He got onto the bike, the movement stretching the denim material over his thighs. Cassie's legs suddenly felt a little rubbery. She realised—as if someone had just punched her—this was *it*. She was experiencing desire. Lust. Attraction. She'd spent years wondering what it must feel like and now she knew. Like a fever.

He was sitting on the bike looking at her, holding out a hand. 'Use me for balance, put your foot—'

'I know,' she said, stepping forward to put the ball of her foot on the footpeg. She ignored his hand, putting hers on his shoulder and stepping up, lifting her other leg over the body of the machine, sitting down.

She slid right down in the hollow between them until her body was flush against his, breasts pressed against his broad back. His very broad and strong back. It felt so much more formidable when she was pressed up against him like this.

He turned his face towards her. 'Wrap your arms around me and hold on.'

Cassie didn't need any encouragement. These last few seconds had been the most exciting of her life to date. She wrapped her arms around his lean torso and with a roar of the throttle that scattered people around them, they were off.

What the hell are you doing, man? The voice in Ares's head wasn't his, it was Caius's, and he scowled inside the helmet. His logic had been: Get the princess out of that situation and then…when she'd been about to walk away it had been: Keep her with you so you know where she is. Keep her safe.

But as he roared along a coastal road now, with her arms around his waist, hands linked together, all too close to a part of his anatomy that was *very* reactive to her proximity, Ares had to admit that his motives had been much more instinctive and less altruistic. Completely unprofessional.

He had sent off a text to Caius though, just before he'd gone over to disrupt the nefarious plans of those idiots, telling his friend that he had located her. And… she was technically under his protection for now.

So yeah, taking her off to a quieter part of the island to have a drink and a dance was totally acceptable. Ares leaned into a turn in the road and her hands tightened around him, making his erection twitch. He gritted his jaw and resisted the urge to take one of her hands and put it between his legs where he throbbed for her. He couldn't remember the last time a woman had turned him on this easily. She was no mere woman. She was a queen in waiting. A totally out-of-bounds woman. And yet, apparently, blonde Disney princesses *were* his type.

Doubts assailed him again. This had been a really stupid idea. He should have just told her who he was and that she was under his protection until her team were back in place. As soon as they stopped, that was what he would do and then he would take her back to her hotel.

The bike stopped and Cassie took the helmet off, shaking out her hair. They were on the edge of a gorgeous little marina/harbour with houses and buildings jostling along the edge, all different colours. Bustling bars and cafes, restaurants. People sitting outside eating and drinking. A very faint sound of disco music coming from the other end of the stretch.

Night had fallen properly now and a crescent moon hung in the sky like a bauble. Stars twinkling.

It was a world away from the over-touristy place she'd been. Using her hand, she balanced on him and got off the bike. Her legs felt wobbly as the adrenalin left her system. She avoided looking at the man as he got off the bike and took off his helmet. She suddenly felt shy. It had been so intimate, wedged up against him, her hands wrapped together just over his—

'Where is this place?' she asked, hoping he wouldn't see how it had affected her.

'It's Rethymno, a little quieter than where we were.'

'It's lovely. Quaint. And yes, quieter, thank you.' She cast a glance at him and felt heat climb into her cheeks. She could remember how flat and hard-muscled his torso had felt under her arms. How she'd wanted to undo her hands and slip one under the material of his shirt.

He said, 'Look, I need to tell you—'

For some reason Cassie didn't want him to finish his sentence. She stuck out a hand and said, 'I'm Cloe.' She mentally crossed her fingers at the white lie, assuring herself that one of her names *was* actually Clotilde, so it wasn't a total untruth.

He looked at her for a long moment and then he took her hand, saying, 'I'm Ares.'

Reluctantly she took her hand out of his, liking it far too much. 'You're Greek?'

He nodded.

She smiled. 'Well, that makes sense. We're in Greece.' She cringed inwardly. She was being an idiot.

Cassie glanced around quickly and said, 'Look, I owe you a drink for potentially saving me from a pretty horrific situation. How about that bar over there?'

He looked to where she was pointing and Cassie held her breath. She could hear some kind of jazzy funky music beat. A world away from the disco inferno they'd just left behind.

After what felt like an eternity, Ares said, 'Sure, after you.'

Relief swept through Cassie. Because this man had single-handedly woken her desire. Like Sleeping Beauty. Cassie suppressed a slightly hysterical giggle. She blinked her eyes a few times. The dark contacts she'd put in were scratching a little but she couldn't drop her guard now. She knew she was being reckless by evading her bodyguards and it was the most rebellious thing she'd ever done, but, that tacky bar earlier aside, this was turning into one of the most thrilling evenings of her life.

Pathetic. She ignored the little voice and stepped into the bar, very aware of the tall solid presence behind her.

Cassie was still a little unused to not being automatically recognised so when the greeter came over and skipped over her to look up at Ares, it was a little jolting but not entirely unwelcome. Ares stood beside her, and as they were led to a table in a corner booth, he lightly touched her back. *Her bare back.*

Electricity sparked up and down her spine and between her legs felt sensitive and hot. She slid into the booth, and he followed her, accepting the menu from the server, who couldn't seem to take her eyes off him. Cassie couldn't blame her.

Sitting beside him now, she could really take him in. The hard planes of his face, that mouth. Deep-set eyes. Softened by the beard that hugged his jaw. Messy hair. He should look thoroughly disreputable but there was something about him that Cassie recognised. *Class.* He couldn't hide that. Intriguing.

He looked at her and she swallowed. She was not used to this at all. 'So, um, do you come from this island?'

He shook his head. 'No, the mainland.'

He hadn't cracked a smile once since they'd met. Cassie smiled for both of them. Being sunny came easily. She'd been doing it all her life. 'Care to narrow it down a bit?'

His gaze was fixed on her mouth and then it moved up over her face. She'd never felt so self-conscious. She was very aware of the heavy make-up, contacts and glitter. He looked as if he was holding back a scowl. Definitely not Mr Charming.

'Athens.'

Then he said, 'What about you?'

Cassie tensed but kept the smile in place, because

it seemed to unnerve him. 'Oh, I'm just here for a few days on holiday.'

'From where?' he all but bit out.

Cassie waved a hand. 'A little place you'll never have heard of, near the South of France.'

Luckily the server came back and took orders for drinks before he asked her to elaborate. Cassie ordered a sparkling wine and Ares ordered something non-alcoholic. When the server left, he put an arm across the back of the seat. Cassie was very aware that his fingers rested within touching distance of the top of her back.

Feeling a little out of her depth but trying to ignore it, she asked, 'So are you here on holiday too?'

He shook his head. 'No, work.'

Cassie made her smile brighter. 'You're not fond of long sentences, are you?'

There was the faintest glimmer in his eyes to show that her remark had made its mark. So maybe there was some humour after all. And why on earth was he so appealing when he wasn't even going out of his way to charm her? Was she hard-wired to be drawn to people who she felt she had to humour? That cut a little too close to the bone and Cassie felt her smile slipping just as the drinks were delivered.

She took a quick sip to hide the sudden onset of introspection. Ares took a sip too of his drink and Cassie couldn't avoid looking at the way his throat moved… leading down to the top of his chest, revealed by a couple of open shirt buttons. She could see dark hair, curling. He was so *male*. She'd never thought she'd find someone so unashamedly masculine attractive.

She put down her drink. 'So, what is your work, then?'

He put down his glass but kept his hand around it. Cassie couldn't help but notice his long fingers, blunt nails. She could just look at him all day. He was mesmerising.

'I dabble in a couple of things...investment, and logistics.'

'Sounds...vague,' Cassie said. He obviously wasn't going to elaborate.

'What about you?'

Cassie fiddled with her glass, avoided his eye. She could be vague too. 'I, um, just graduated university not long ago.' That was true. She'd graduated from the main university on Sadat Sur Mer.

'What did you study?'

'Economics and international relations. And languages.' Except she'd been speaking at least four languages fluently since she was a child.

'You're not working yet?' he asked.

She'd been working her whole life as a princess, but he couldn't know that. Cassie crossed her fingers on her lap, under the table. 'I'm actually starting a new job within the next few weeks, hence this holiday.'

Ares arched a brow. 'I guess that's as good a time as any for a holiday.'

Relieved he wasn't asking for more information on her *job*, and worried where the conversation might stray next, Cassie blurted out, 'Would you like to dance?'

He looked at her and drew back slightly. Cassie's

insides dropped. Had that been a really gauche thing to do? She was so inexperienced at this. She'd always been so protected and cosseted, and, even if she'd liked a guy, they were usually so intimidated by who she was that they wouldn't come near her. In a way she could understand now why Caius had socialised with the people he had, because it simply would have been too awkward not to.

But suddenly Ares said, 'Yes, OK.' And he was sliding out of the booth and holding out his hand.

CHAPTER THREE

What the hell are you doing, man? You were meant to tell her who you were as soon as you arrived. This is such a bad idea, tell her now—but at the feel of Cassie's small hand sliding into his, all of Ares's thoughts stopped dead.

This had to be better than sitting next to her and breathing in her evocative scent, musky and flowery and earthy all at once. It had taken all of his control not to let his fingers touch her hair, test if it felt as silky as it looked. Even with those lurid colours through it, nothing could dim the golden blonde strands.

He led her to the small space where other couples had moved together as the music changed and became more sultry. He turned and faced her. She was taller than he'd expected her to be. Even without the heels she'd be above average height.

He tugged her towards him and she came with a tiny stumble that brought her flush with his body. She was all slim, lithe curves and her breasts pressed against his chest. He already knew they were bigger than he might have first thought because he'd seen her cleavage, unwittingly presented when she'd folded her arms in front of him. And then, on the bike, pressed against him. She wore no bra. The thought of those perfect orbs of flesh, loose and unbound—Ares gritted his jaw to try and maintain some semblance of control as he spread his hand across her back.

She felt incredibly delicate and yet there was a latent strength. He had a sense not to underestimate her. After all, she'd managed to ditch her bodyguards and avoid her brother.

He looked down at her and she lifted her face. She smiled. It made something inside Ares ache. Why was she so smiley? So perky? She was a princess way out of her depth. She could have been unconscious somewhere now if it hadn't been for him. But again he had that sense that perhaps she would have surprised him by managing to get out of that predicament. She was using a false name to avoid detection.

Then his gaze went to her mouth. It opened slightly and he had a glimpse of pink tongue. White teeth. A fire started raging in his blood. He'd never been more tempted by a woman. By a woman who was so far out of his bounds that—

Before Ares could formulate another word, she'd reached up and pressed her mouth to his, a chaste and surprisingly sweet gesture. But any thought of *sweet* fast dissolved as the kiss morphed into burning hot heat and intense need. Ares couldn't resist. Didn't want to resist. So he didn't.

Cassie's heart was thumping so hard she felt sure the entire island must be able to hear it. One minute she'd been looking up into that gorgeous face, at that provocatively sexy mouth, and the next she'd done the most audacious thing. She'd kissed him, reaching up on tippy-toe. Winding her arms around his neck.

His mouth had felt hard and unyielding under hers. Warm but unmoving. *She'd made a bad mistake. This guy wasn't remotely into her at all.* She'd been about to pull back, her insides curdling with humiliation, and she'd taken a breath against his lips and then everything had changed.

He'd reciprocated. No. He'd taken over. Masterfully. Pulling her even closer with his arms, welding her to him so tight that she swore she could feel every ridge of his hard musculature. His arms were like steel. And she *loved it*.

His mouth moved over hers now, coaxing a response that Cassie gave instinctively. She had been kissed before but she'd always had to make the move because guys were so intimidated and then nothing much had happened. They'd been like deer in the headlights. Those experiences had only reinforced her impression that perhaps she wasn't destined for a life of passion. But now…she was being given a crash course.

Ares's tongue touched hers and an electric shock went straight to between her legs. She pressed her thighs together as if that could contain the sense of burgeoning tension and excitement.

The kiss deepened and became explicit. Testing, tasting. Luxuriating. It was as if they had all the time in the world for this exquisite pleasure. Bodies pressed together, tongues duelling.

Slowly, Cassie realised that her back was against a wall. Ares had manoeuvred them off the main floor to a corner near the booth.

He broke the kiss and lifted his head. Cassie felt drunk. It took an age for her to be able to open her eyes. And he was blurry at first and then came back into focus. Her mouth was tingling, and between her legs felt swollen and hot and damp.

As if reading her mind, he inserted a thigh between her legs and Cassie almost whimpered as the movement caused a friction that made her bite her lip. She wanted to rub against him, to alleviate the building tension.

He put his hands on her waist and his hands and the wall were the only things holding her up. He shook his head. 'You are…a temptress.'

Cassie felt like giggling. But then she didn't as one of his hands moved up over her waist, tracing the curve, moving closer and closer to the underside of her breast. And then she sucked in a breath, all thoughts of giggling gone as his hand cupped the weight of her breast. And then his thumb moved back and forth across one tight and tingling nipple.

Cassie's thighs tightened around Ares's and she felt a flutter of sensation at her core. She was holding onto his arms and she couldn't reach all the way around they were so thickly muscled.

She felt primitive. Him man, her woman. She wanted to climb him and wrap her legs around him.

She said, without even really thinking, 'Please, Ares, touch me, show me...how it can be.'

He cupped her breast more firmly and bent his head and captured her mouth in another searing hot kiss. Deep and explicit straight away, no leading into it. Cassie welcomed it, wrapping her arms around him again, opening herself up to his hands, inviting him to touch her, moving against him in a way that had her starting to gasp with need as an elusive peak shimmered in the distance.

Ares's hand on her breast squeezed hard, fingers trapping a nipple. Cassie suddenly wanted more, wanted to feel his mouth on her there, surrounding that tight peak in heat and moisture.

Ares took his thigh from between hers and replaced it with his hand. He cupped her through the soft denim, right there over where she throbbed. He moved his hand against her, watching her. Cassie felt a little exposed because he oozed such confidence and experience but suddenly she stopped thinking because she was pressing against his hand and he was moving in a rhythmic motion and a force she'd never felt before held her body in an alien grip before it exploded into a rush of pleasure so intense that she would have called out loud if he hadn't taken her mouth again and swallowed her orgasmic cry.

The world and reality came back slowly. The sounds of the bar, music. People laughing. Cassie was grateful that Ares was shielding her from everyone else. No one would know that she'd just had her first orgasm with a total stranger in a bar in Crete. *Ares*. Not a total stranger. But as good as.

A million and one things were rushing through Cassie as this sank in. Ares seemed to be watching her warily as if she were a bomb about to go off. She had just gone off, against his hand. Heat climbed into her face. She was glad of the dark.

He put his hands on her arms and somehow, sensing a shift in the mood, Cassie managed to straighten up. Her legs were still working. Albeit wobbly. He must think she was so gauche.

'I…' Her tongue felt thick as she tried to formulate something.

Ares shook his head. 'You don't have to say anything. Not a word. This is on me. My fault.'

Cassie felt a trickle of unease trace down her spine. That was an odd thing to say. 'What do you mean, your fault?'

He let her arms go and took a step back. Ran a hand through his hair, making it messier. He looked at her. 'Because we should never have come here.'

Something occurred to Cassie and she reared back. 'You're married.'

A look of disgust crossed his face. '*Theos*, no. I'm not married.'

Cassie was confused. 'You have a girlfriend?'

The disgust again. '*No*. I don't *do* girlfriends.'

He took her arm in his hand and had started to guide her back out of the bar, through the couples mingling and dancing, before Cassie even knew what was happening.

When they were outside and fresh air hit her, she stopped, forcing him to stop too. 'What are you doing?'

He let her go and looked at her. 'We need to leave.'

Something about the return of that censorious tone and the fact that *he* had decided to leave stung Cassie somewhere vulnerable. Had she been such a bad kisser? Had her orgasm been such a faux pas? A turn-off? The expression on his face hadn't been disgusted or bored, it had been intense. But had she imagined that?

She felt even more exposed. 'You might have decided that you no longer want to stay here but that's your decision.'

He gritted his jaw. He really was such a taciturn man. Cassie wondered what on earth she found attractive about him. *Everything.* She wanted to scowl. She'd certainly found him pretty attractive just a few minutes ago. Her body still felt hot inside, as if something had melted.

'I brought you here, I'll take you back.'

Now she was offended. 'Charming, like a parcel you've suddenly decided you no longer want.'

She tossed her hair and drew herself up to her full height, which was still a good few inches short of his. In heels. 'You don't have to *take* me anywhere, Ares. I've decided I like this bar and I'm staying. Goodnight.'

She turned and went to walk back into the bar, her insides fizzing and jumping with a mixture of hurt, confusion and anger, when from behind her she heard, 'It's not that simple, princess.'

Cassie's feet stopped. She wondered if she'd heard that right. *Princess.* Surely she was just being paranoid, he'd meant it as some sort of figure of speech. Inappropriate though, because clearly he had no interest in her and was just trying to salve his conscience now by returning her to where he'd picked her up. But it was still weird.

She turned around. 'What did you call me?'

'Princess.'

Her insides tightened. This man was a total stranger, he couldn't possibly—

'Princess Cassandra Mansur de Roche. Crown Princess, to be precise. You'll have to forgive me for not remembering your middle names, there are quite a few, but I'm assuming Cloe is one of them.'

For a moment Cassie heard nothing but a dull roaring sound, and then she was suddenly light-headed. She was going to faint. *No.* He moved towards her as if sensing her shock. She put up a hand between them, as the full enormity of what this meant rushed through her brain and body with a million and one ramifications hitting her all at once.

He said, 'I'm not from the press or anything like that. I'm a friend of your brother's. He sent me to track you down because he was worried about you.'

Cassie felt a flash of anger at her brother for interfering when she didn't need him and for not being around when she did need him. She knew there was no point denying who she was. 'I've taken some time off. He doesn't need to be worried. I told him I was OK.'

'But not where you were. If he'd seen what I saw

earlier he would have had reason to be worried.' Admonishing her when a moment ago she'd been all but climbing him like a tree and orgasming into his cupped hand.

Cassie felt her blood start to boil, eclipsing the shock. This man had known who she was and hadn't been fully honest with her.

'For your information, Mr Ares Whatever Your Second Name Is, I'm skilled in self-defence, I've been taking classes since I was small so I would have been absolutely *fine*.'

'Not if you'd been unconscious due to a drug in the drink. And my second name is Drakos, Ares Drakos.'

It suited him, she thought a little churlishly, curt and abrupt like him. 'I wasn't going to take the drink. I didn't trust them.'

'You trusted me.'

Cassie folded her arms at the humiliating reminder and it struck her then that perhaps, somewhere deep down, she'd suspected that he wasn't just some gorgeous man who'd appeared as her guardian angel. Ha! Guardian devil.

The sense of exposure was compounded now by feeling acutely self-conscious. She'd allowed herself to believe him to be a total stranger who had been overcome with lust for her. She'd revealed herself to him in ways she'd never done with anyone else. He'd brought her to orgasm. In public.

Mortification and the heat of shame crawled upwards through her body. 'You should have told me you knew who I was.'

'Yes,' he said immediately, 'I should have. It was a lapse of judgement.'

Cassie was a little taken aback by his straightforward admission of guilt. She frowned, thinking of something belatedly. 'Why did my brother call you?'

'I own a private security company. I will stay with you until your bodyguards have you under their protection again.'

Cassie shook her head and started to back away. 'No, you won't. We're done here, Mr Drakos. You found me and you had your fun at my expense.'

She looked around, feeling panicky. She needed to get away from this man and those dark eyes and that unsmiling face. And that mouth and those hands that had played her like an instrument for his amusement.

She saw a line of taxis about a hundred feet away and she walked quickly towards them. From behind her she heard, 'Princess Cassandra, wait.'

But she didn't turn around, she jumped into the back of the first taxi and, with her heart hammering and her insides tight with humiliation and embarrassment, she gave the address of her hotel.

She looked out of the window as the taxi turned to go in the right direction. He was standing there, a tall, powerful figure. And everything they'd just shared was tainted. He knew who and where she was now, her peace was shattered. In more ways than one.

She never wanted to see that man again.

CHAPTER FOUR

CASSIE HAD SENT her brother a text when she'd returned to her hotel last night.

Caius, I'm fine, please let me have this time to myself. You had your years of freedom. In a matter of weeks, I'll no longer have this luxury. I love you. x Cass.

Cassie hadn't received a response from Caius. But she knew that didn't mean much. He knew where she was now. He'd sent his *friend* after her. His friend, who when she'd looked him up online last night had suddenly appeared in numerous photos with her brother, coming out of various bars and clubs going back a few years.

It didn't look as if he'd been any happier in those moments, a stern, or even scowling, counterpoint to Caius's playboy-prince mischievous grin. Cassie had generally avoided looking at her brother's exploits online, naturally enough.

But if she had, then Ares Drakos might have been familiar to her last night. Because clearly he'd enjoyed playing the playboy along with her brother and apart from pictures of him with Caius there had been plenty of him at glittering functions with a stunning woman on his arm. A different one every time. Blonde, brunette, redhead. He didn't seem to have a type. Maybe he was just the kind of guy who would hook up at any opportunity. With any willing woman.

Like last night. Cassie had to push down the resurgence of humiliation that had kept her awake with heartburn all night.

Ares Drakos was from one of Greece's biggest shipping dynasties and yet he'd broken relations with his family when he'd graduated high school, at the age of seventeen. He'd turned his back on his inheritance and the family business to go his own way.

He'd served with the Greek army before going into the special forces for a few years, but those details were hazy. There were several online rumours that he'd been involved in some of the most high-profile security engagements in the world, including several political prisoner swaps.

He'd emerged from his time with security forces and set up his own security company—Drakos Security. There was little information about it online except for the mention that Ares had invested in cutting-edge software that had made his security company one of the most in demand in the world. And worth billions.

Cassie huffed to herself now that he'd probably used this *software* to track her down.

She was dressed today in cut-off shorts, sneakers and a T-shirt that she'd tied in a knot at her waist. Her hair was now free of the temporary tie-dyed colours and up and stuffed under a baseball cap. She didn't have contacts in her eyes to disguise their colour.

She'd leased a sailing boat from a marina on the other side of the island. She was going to avoid any more troublesome interactions by taking to the seas and doing some island hopping.

That would give her space to think and enjoy her freedom. *Alone.* She ignored the pang of loneliness.

Well, she thought to herself as she jumped down from the boat to the wooden walkway to untie it, *better alone than being potentially drugged or mocked.*

She had the rope in her hand and she was about to step back onto the boat when the skin on the back of her neck prickled and she went still.

No.

Slowly she turned around to see an all too familiar tall, broad figure just a few feet away. He was wearing board shorts and a short-sleeved polo shirt. He had a baseball cap too and it shadowed his face but she could still make out the hard, bearded jaw and that provocative mouth.

In fractured moments of sleep last night she'd dreamt of that mouth. Touching more than her lips.

'What are you doing here?' As she asked that question she noticed that he was carrying a scuffed holdall. She pointed to it. 'What is that?'

He lifted it up and Cassie noticed the way his muscles bulged. She also remembered how hard his chest had felt against hers.

He said, 'It's my bag. I'm coming with you.'

Panic spiked. Cassie turned away and jumped

lithely onto the boat. She turned to face him. 'No, you're not.'

He walked to where there was one more rope mooring the boat to the dock and he put his foot on top of the post, Cassie cursed inwardly.

'Yes, I am. Your brother has acquired my services until such time as you're done with this little trip and you're back at the palace.'

Cassie shook her head. 'No way, no how. He has no right to do this. I'll pay you double whatever he's paying you to leave me alone.'

'It's not about the money. He's my friend and it's a personal favour.'

Cassie smiled sweetly, belying the way her belly was cramping with tension. 'Well, we were pretty friendly last night, maybe you'll do me a personal favour and get lost?' She had never been so rude in her life. But something about standing up to this man was a little shamefully exhilarating, especially when she'd spent all her life trying to make everyone else happy.

Now he smiled and Cassie almost fell off the boat. His mouth was wide and his teeth were very white and the smile completely transformed his face. Even though she knew it wasn't a real smile. Lord help her if he ever did that. She scowled. She wasn't going to ever see him smile for real and didn't want to.

She secured the rope in her hand and went back down onto the walkway to untie the last rope mooring the boat to the jetty. She looked expressly at his foot and tried not to be so aware of his size. 'Can you move your foot, please?'

'Not until you tell me where you plan on going.'

She looked up from under the rim of her cap. 'Island hopping, not that it's any of your business. But after last night I'd prefer to take my chances with sharks at sea rather than the sharks on land.'

She bent down and pushed his foot off the bollard and lifted up the rope, moving back towards the boat. She hadn't even unbalanced him.

'I'm coming with you whether you like it or not, sweetheart.'

Cassie went rigid and turned back towards him. 'I am not your *sweetheart*. And I am leaving now on this boat. If you attempt to board I will call the marina police and have you arrested.'

'And how will that look in the papers, hm? Crown Princess Cassandra running from her duties to be queen?'

Cassie's mouth fell open and her eyes widened. 'You wouldn't dare.'

He shrugged one wide shoulder. 'I've been given a brief and I don't ever renege on an assignment and my assignment is you until you're back at the palace under the protection of your own guards again, who, admittedly, need a refresher course in how to protect you.'

My assignment is you. Those words sent more than a frisson of awareness into Cassie's blood.

'Now,' he said, 'we're not leaving here on a boat. I have a private plane standing by ready to take you wherever you'd like, preferably back to your palace but if you insist on wanting to island hop then that's what we'll do.'

A million things buzzed into Cassie's head—the sheer arrogance for one, that censorious tone again along with a trace of weariness, as if suffering a petulant child.

She very deliberately stepped back onto the boat that was now untethered from the jetty and, after securing the rope, she stood up with hands on her hips. 'Now,' she said, mimicking his tone, 'I am not leaving here, except on this boat that I have paid good money for. I have no desire to contribute to global warming by using a private jet when I don't have to. There's an app that you can download that'll allow you to follow the boat's progress—feel free to keep an eye on me that way. I'd really prefer it.'

Cassie turned her back on Ares and focused on turning the engine on to navigate out of the marina. She couldn't see someone like Ares Drakos dancing to her tune, so good riddance.

Ares looked at the boat and the back of Crown Princess Cassandra as she stood by one of the two big wheels. It had taken more strength than he cared to admit just to walk down the jetty to where she had been untying the boat. Not even her long, golden, slim legs and that high, curvy behind encased in demin could have stopped the clammy feeling of sweat on his brow and palms.

Or the bolt of electricity he'd felt when she'd looked up at him from under her cap and he'd seen those amazing blue eyes that she'd hidden under contacts last night.

He hated boats. Loathed them. *He still had nightmares about them.*

He'd been kidnapped when he was ten and the gang had held him on a boat, moving around to evade detection, as they'd negotiated with his parents for his return.

His parents had fought paying up, fearing it would set a precedent, caring more for their vast wealth and reputation than the life of one son. They'd had another heir in his older brother, Axel, so they could afford to lose one.

Axel's academic prowess in contrast to Ares's struggles reading and writing had ensured that Ares was never going to inherit the family business, highlighted by the reaction to his kidnapping.

In the end, it had been a specialist team from the police department who had tracked down the boat and saved Ares, with no help from his family. It had shown Ares that the police force had cared more than his own flesh and blood about his welfare.

He'd returned home, traumatised and changed for ever. His brother had wanted to know what had happened but Ares hadn't been able to talk about it. And his parents had encouraged him not to talk about it. To just forget. Eventually Axel had stopped asking and had been drawn more and more into the realm of becoming successor to their father—cementing an even bigger gulf between the brothers.

His sisters had been too young and Ares had distanced himself from them too, finding their childish innocence terrifying—because he knew how quickly it could be taken away.

He'd vowed to make sure he was never that vulnerable again, by taking care of himself. It had been clear his family hadn't valued him as worth protecting, so as soon as he was of age, he'd left.

He'd also vowed to do his utmost to help those who needed it. Those who were left behind, forgotten by the ones who should be protecting them.

That was why he really, really resented his time being taken away from a more worthwhile cause than caretaking a wayward princess. And why he hated boats so much.

In spite of which, he knew how to sail, because his father hadn't allowed Ares's traumatic experience to be the reason he couldn't take control of a boat. It had simply been unconscionable that, as the son of a shipping magnate, a Drakos couldn't handle a boat and so he'd spent his teens white-knuckling and sweating his way through being forced to sail on many occasions.

But Ares had only been on water in recent years if it was absolutely necessary for a security mission. To save a life. Certainly not on the whim of a big brother who wanted his little sister protected at all costs. No matter how much he liked the guy.

She's not just anyone, a voice pointed out. *She's a crown princess, about to become a head of state.*

That held no sway with Ares. She wanted to have her cake and eat it. Privilege *and* freedom. She needed his protection about as much as a tiger did. Her biggest danger was making eyes at goons who would want to spike her drink. *Or going off with a stranger who then ravished her in a public place at the first opportunity.*

Ares's conscience stung. He couldn't put that on her. It had been all him and his wayward libido. The sun must have got to him yesterday.

Then he heard the engine revving and his tension spiked. He realised she had every intention of pulling out of this marina and leaving. In the midst of his churning guts he had to hand it to her. She wasn't afraid of him. *Because she expects you to jump to her bidding.*

Whatever. Ares wasn't here to pass judgement on her. He knew he had no choice. He would have to dance to her tune. For now. He swallowed down the rising panic and gritted his jaw before jumping lithely onto the boat, just as it started to move away from the jetty.

Ares swayed a little on the boat as it picked up speed out of the marina and gulped down more nausea. At least he wasn't deep below deck this time, locked into a tiny cabin.

At that moment Princess Cassandra looked around from the wheel and scowled at him from under her cap. Ares arranged his face into a smile that felt more like a grimace and said, 'I haven't had a holiday in years. This'll be fun.'

About thirty minutes later, Cassie's heart was still thudding. He was on the boat with her. In her peripheral vision on the seats that encased the deck where she was standing at the wheel. She was suddenly annoyed she hadn't hired a much bigger boat. This felt very intimate even though it was a family-sized sailing boat with a generous cabin area down below.

There was a compact kitchen, stocked with supplies, and a dining/seating area. A master cabin was in the bow with a small en suite, and two more small bedrooms and the head/toilet at the stern of the boat.

She was sure he'd get off at the first stop. He was just calling her bluff. But shamefully her dominant reactions weren't anger or frustration, they were something more like anticipation, *excitement*. She scowled into the warm Aegean breeze, trying to focus on navigating.

Ares Drakos was a busy man, no way was he going to settle for babysitting her, no matter how close to Caius he was.

That piqued her curiosity, in spite of herself. Caius gave off the impression of being charming and amenable and the life and soul of the party but Cassie knew well that he used that to deflect from the fact that, actually, he was a lot more serious and guarded than he wanted anyone to know.

So the fact that her brother obviously trusted Ares Drakos was intriguing to say the least.

She and Caius had both been affected by their parents' chaotic and destructive relationship and she knew that it had had a profound impact on Caius to find out that the king hadn't been his father. She could only imagine what that knowledge would do to your sense of yourself—suddenly finding out you weren't who you thought you were. The fact that he was still trying to protect her even though he'd had to step aside made her conscience prick. It hadn't been his fault that their world had shifted on its axis like this.

Then, just when she'd almost convinced herself that she was actually alone and not with a taciturn uninvited guest, Ares's voice came over the throb of the engine. 'So, I presume you know what you're doing if you're sailing this boat by yourself?'

Cassie glanced at him reluctantly and hated the way her heart skipped a beat. He was sitting, legs sprawled, bag on the seat beside him. Arms out across the back of the seat. For all the world as if he had chartered the boat and she were just an employee.

She wasn't used to people making her feel prickly and she didn't like it. 'We'll soon find out, won't we?'

She turned back to face the horizon as he said, 'Wouldn't it have been easier to hire a catamaran with a crew? Plenty of space to lounge about and work on your tan.'

Cassie made sure the chart plotter was set with the right coordinates and turned back to face Ares and folded her arms, glad she was wearing more clothes this time. Well, apart from her cut-off shorts.

'My aim was to take this boat trip *alone*.'

Ares took off his baseball cap and ran a hand through his hair, making it even messier. And was his jaw even more stubbled today? But did he look a little pale under his tan? Green, even? Eyes a bit pinched? He seemed supremely relaxed but Cassie could sense a very subtle tension in his form. Before she could wonder about it too much he said, 'Don't you have any friends to play with?'

Cassie's hackles reached nuclear levels because he was unwittingly highlighting the fact again that she was alone and hadn't anticipated feeling this... *lonely*. At all. She did have friends; they just had pretty normal lives and weren't available to go sailing on a whim.

She gritted out, 'Not that it's any business of yours, but I do have friends. Good ones. And maybe I want to be alone to gather my thoughts.'

'Ah yes, no doubt to contemplate the new job you alluded to last night, becoming Queen of Sadat Sur Mer.'

Casssie's jaw gritted even more. 'You mean last night when I was led to believe you had no idea who I was?'

He had the grace to look sheepish. 'I told you that was a mistake. You had a right to know who I was.'

'Yes, I did. But clearly it was far too tempting to mock me and make a fool of me.' Cassie was surprised at the depth of emotion that spiked. As if he'd somehow had the power to hurt her by deceiving her.

She turned back to the horizon that was wide and empty except for little smudges of other boats and islands in the far distance.

'I'm sorry.'

She tensed, wondering if she'd heard right. Then his voice came again. 'My intent was not to deceive you, princess. I mean that.'

Cassie hated the way his apology made her tension dissipate. She glanced at him, and now he was sitting forward with his hands linked between wide-apart legs.

'So why did you?' And then she added, 'And don't call me princess. My name is Cassie.'

Last night she'd told him, *I'm Cloe.* She pushed the memory aside.

He looked as if he was gritting his teeth and then he said, 'Cassie.'

He couldn't be further from the intense brooding stranger from last night who had enveloped her in his strength and heat, coaxing her to a climax before she'd even realised what was happening. And he also didn't seem inclined to answer her question.

'Look,' she said eventually, 'I'm heading for Santorini. I'll drop anchor and bring you to the island on the tender. You can make your own way from there. You obviously don't want to be here and I don't need babysitting.' *You are going to be a queen.* Cassie could almost hear Pierre's scandalised voice in her head.

But Ares was already shaking his head anyway. 'No can do. While you're insisting on taking this little pleasure trip, I'm by your side.' He sat back again and regarded her. It was patently obvious that he judged her as selfish and spoiled.

Little pleasure trip. He riled her up so easily, it was a little scary. She knew she shouldn't let him get to her but she was putting hands on her hips and facing him. 'Did you ever judge my brother like this when you and he met up on *your* little pleasure trips to exclusive nightclubs and bars?'

He had the grace to flush slightly. Cassie felt ridiculously pleased that she could get to him.

He said, 'You looked me up.'

Cassie faced back to the sea, hands on the wheel. 'Of course I did. It's only because I don't snoop on my brother's social activities that I didn't recognise you, but now that I know you share his playboy...proclivities, last night makes a lot of sense. But if I had known who you were I wouldn't have let you come within five feet of me.'

Ares surged up from the seat in her peripheral vision and Cassie tightened her hands around the wheel. She looked at him. His face was dark.

He bit out, 'I am not a playboy.'

Cassie shivered a little inside. He was *so* intense. It called to that part of her deep down underneath where she'd resented having to be the sunny antidote to the animosity around her growing up.

Feeling as if she were playing with a great white shark, she said, 'If it walks like a duck and quacks like a duck...'

'Those pictures with your brother were only taken because it's impossible to go anywhere with him without being tailed by paparazzi. We met for drinks. Maybe once or twice went clubbing together.'

Cassie was intrigued. She'd hit a nerve. He didn't like being associated with her brother's more debauched behaviour. Which admittedly hadn't been that debauched. He'd just developed a reputation for being seen at every exclusive glittering event and blazing a trail through Europe's most beautiful women, each of whom had desperately wanted to be his queen. Until they'd invariably found themselves waking alone in a bed long gone cold.

'So you didn't leave a string of broken-hearted lovers behind you like my brother did? All that means is you're more discreet.' That reminded her of how he'd been careful to shield her from the people in the bar last night. As she'd orgasmed. She turned away again, face getting hot.

Cassie said, 'My point is that you're allowed to go out clubbing, Ares, and so am I, if I feel like it. Maybe I'll try a couple in Santorini.'

'What exactly is it you're hoping to get out of this trip?'

Cassie felt exposed. How could she articulate to this unsmiling man that being crowned queen both excited her and terrified her? It would make the world her gilded prison. She would never have this chance again to try and be incognito and to try to taste some of the freedom her brother had been afforded because he'd naturally had a less restricted life just because he'd been a man.

It had almost been expected of him to carouse and make mayhem before settling down. Double standards. She didn't hold it against her brother, and she knew that his hectic social whirl had largely been a smokescreen to deflect from his own inner demons.

But that hadn't been her scene and it was only now she was realising what she'd missed out on. A chance to feel free and unburdened. As much as someone like her could. A chance to live an alternate existence for a while. A chance to live for her twin. No, she couldn't articulate all that to this man.

Cassie ignored his question. 'I saw that you came from one of Greece's most prominent shipping dynasties.'

Silence and then, after a long moment he responded with, 'It's no secret.'

'Nor does it seem to be a secret that you walked away from your inheritance at a young age.'

'Yes.' Clipped. Not inviting more comment.

Cassie looked at Ares from under her baseball cap. 'Well, I don't have that luxury. It's not as if I want to walk away, in any case. I'm happy to do my duty as Queen of Sadat. It's an honour and a privilege. But is it so bad to want to experience a little window of freedom before it's gone for good?'

Ares had no answer for that. He hadn't really considered the full reality of what she was facing. A life of duty. Being beholden to a nation, even a small one. Having to watch every step you took and word you said for fear of bringing scandal or infamy on your people.

Caius had worn that responsibility lightly and Ares had to admit now, a little uncomfortably, that his decadent behaviour had been all but sanctioned—he'd just been living up to his playboy reputation and making the most of it before his life changed.

Ares had seen glimpses of a much more serious Caius, hiding behind the flashing paparazzi lights, but they hadn't ever strayed into deeper emotional territory. There wouldn't have been enough whiskey in the world for that level of bonding. They'd both tacitly acknowledged that they had their own *stuff* and had skirted around it.

He could imagine the rolling of Cassie's eyes if he were to admit that. Strange, he'd only known her for less than twenty-four hours yet he felt he knew her better than others he'd known for years. *You made her come against your hand.*

Ares's body reacted to that provocative thought. He had felt jealous of his hand, last night. He'd wanted to be embedded deep inside her and he'd wanted to feel the pulsing strength of her orgasm around him, milking him.

The fact that she'd looked him up online made him feel exposed. He knew she wouldn't have seen anything of the kidnapping as his family had managed to all but expunge the unsavoury episode from the records to protect their reputation. But it was still there, in corners of the Internet. She obviously hadn't dug that deep.

Ares was grateful. The thought of her knowing about that…made him feel even more exposed. And something he hadn't felt in a very long time. Vulnerable.

He took a step back. 'Fine, Santorini it is.' He had to acknowledge now that the fact that she was helming her own boat without any crew or entourage contradicted his assumptions about her.

She stepped away from the wheel and control panel and said, 'I'm going down to do some unpacking while the coast is clear.'

'I'll keep watch up here.' Ares had very little intention of going anywhere near the below-deck area unless it was absolutely necessary.

'The boat is set on its course. I won't be long.' She came out from behind the big wheel and ducked down into the lower-deck area. Ares let out a breath and ran his hand through his hair again. This was going to be a long week, unless he could convince her to return home sooner.

But strangely that no longer had a sense of urgency about it. He had to concede that her desire for a slice of freedom before taking on a mammoth role wasn't completely unreasonable. And her brother had certainly taken advantage of his.

You could have one of your most trusted employees take over from you in Santorini. Ares knew he could. Caius would be OK with that, if it was still one of Ares's team. But for some reason, Ares wasn't reaching for his phone to make the call. And he wasn't about to investigate why. The fact that he wasn't taking the first opportunity to get off this boat was disturbing enough.

CHAPTER FIVE

'WHY SANTORINI?'

Cassie wondered if she could ignore the question. Ares had insisted on coming with her onto the island. He'd seemed almost eager to get off the boat. She was regretting saying they'd walk the famous almost six hundred steps up from the old port to Fira instead of taking the cable car.

They'd docked the tender at the port. Donkeys meandered up and down the steps carrying luggage and, sometimes, people. One passed her by now with a tourist on its back. Cassie felt sorry for the poor donkey.

She glanced at the man who was keeping pace beside her easily. She noted there wasn't a hint of perspiration or exertion on his face, when hers felt as if it were about to melt off under the seam of the baseball cap she was wearing for protection from the late afternoon sun as much to hide her identity.

She'd changed out of the cut-off shorts and T-shirt into loose linen trousers and a sleeveless V-necked silk top. A bag containing water and other essentials was slung across her body.

'Because I've never been and I've heard the sunset viewed from Oia is spectacular.'

'It's just a sunset.'

Cassie stopped near the top—mercifully—and looked at him. 'Are you always this grumpy or is it my unique effect on you?' she asked and smiled sweetly.

He just scowled behind his dark shades that made him look like a movie star. After Cassie had unpacked earlier and returned up top on the boat, Ares had gone down into the cabin with his bag. She'd called after him with only a modicum of sarcasm, 'Feel free to use one of the rooms at the stern of the boat.'

He hadn't answered. But he had changed into a white short-sleeved polo shirt that made him look even darker and only emphasised his outsize muscles.

It wasn't just the climb up from the port that made her breathless. She went back to climbing the last steps and said, 'If you don't want to be here so badly why don't you send someone else? Maybe they'll be a bit more excited about a sunset.'

Cassie had more or less resigned herself to the fact that she would be shadowed for this trip, whether she liked it or not. She didn't fancy her chances of evading Ares or one of his staff, after reading about him and his company.

'All my staff are busy on assignment.'

Cassie sent Ares a look. 'No doubt protecting far more worthy clients.'

He seemed to stiffen. 'I never said you weren't worthy.'

'You didn't have to,' Cassie said without any rancour. She was actually finding it quite refreshing being around someone who wasn't overly obsequious. Or who she felt she needed to keep happy.

They were at the top of the steps now and Cassie saw a bus being loaded up with *Oia* in the window. She was heading for it when a hand—a large hand—wrapped around her bare upper arm. An electrical charge jolted through her body. She stopped and looked at Ares.

He said, 'Where are you going?'

'Taking the bus to Oia. It's the best place to see the sun set.'

He shook his head. 'No, we'll take a cab.' He was all but herding her to the taxi rank nearby and within a nanosecond she was installed in the back seat with him alongside her, one long muscled thigh far too close for comfort.

He was giving instructions to the driver in Greek and then the car was on the move.

A little stunned at the speed with which the man moved for someone so big and imposing, Cassie said churlishly, 'This is *my* trip.'

'And you're my responsibility. When we're off the boat, I'll dictate the modes of transport.'

'Yes, sir,' Cassie said under her breath.

But obviously not far enough under because he said, 'That's more like it.'

She looked at him but his face was turned away towards his window. She could have sworn she saw the faintest upturn of one side of his mouth and that sent a wave of heat undulating through her body.

Disgusted with herself for being so weak and susceptible to a pretty face and a few bulging muscles, she looked out of her own window.

'This place is like a theme park.'

The words were gritted out from above Cassie's shoulder. She'd taken off her baseball cap and it hung from the strap of her bag. Her hair was pulled back and she was wearing shades. She knew that she more or less blended pretty well with the rest of the tourists. If anything, Ares was the one attracting all the attention, moving through the throngs of people clogging the narrow pretty streets of Oia lined with shops and boutiques and restaurants.

That suited her fine. She loved this sensation of being anonymous among crowds. Then she spotted something and exclaimed, 'Ooh, I was going to try and find this—it's here!'

She veered to the left and heard a stifled curse from behind her. She ducked into the famous bookshop that was situated in a cave that had been turned into a building. Like many of the buildings built into the caldera walls of Santorini.

'It's a...bookshop.'

She turned around to face Ares. He looked stunned as he took it in. No doubt he'd expected her to make for the first exclusive boutique or jewellery store. She was interested in those too but she liked confounding him.

'I've always wanted to see this place.' Cassie wandered further in and gazed at the shelves and poetry written on the walls. It was quirky and coming down with books. Heaven.

She picked up a big glossy hardback of photos of Greece. She could sense Ares's tension beside her and glanced up. 'Look, if you—' She stopped talking when she saw the expression on his face. It looked pained.

She put the book down. 'What is it?'

He shook his head, expression clearing. 'Nothing, I'll wait outside.' He slipped his shades back on and ducked back out through the small doorway. After a few more minutes' browsing, Cassie followed him outside to find him leaning against a wall, hands in his pockets.

He looked relaxed but she could see the tension in those impressive muscles. He saw her and stood up straight. They resumed walking along the street. When it became clear that he wasn't going to elaborate, Cassie asked, 'What was that about?'

'What?'

Cassie rolled her eyes. He was being obtuse. 'You know very well—you looked as if you'd just eaten a side of cold suet pudding.'

The faintest glimmer of a smile touched the corner of his mouth. 'Suet?'

Now Cassie's mouth twitched. 'A particularly revolting dessert we used to be served in boarding scool.'

She felt him glance at her and he said, 'Boarding school?'

She nodded. 'Since I was eight, in Switzerland. I came home for holidays and half-term. But my parents let me do the baccalaureate in Sadat.'

He seemed to digest this and Cassie had resigned herself to him dodging her initial question when he said, 'I'm dyslexic. So...being surrounded by books makes me a little uncomfortable.'

Cassie felt a little punch to her gut at that admission. 'There are so many more ways to read now.'

He shook his head. 'I know, but not so much when I was growing up. My parents weren't very willing to accept that a child of theirs was in any way imperfect.'

Cassie stopped in the narrow street, forcing people to swerve and go around them. She put her hands on her hips, filled with indignation. 'That's outrageous. Some of the most successful people on the planet have dyslexia. If anything it means you're above average because you've had to mask or engineer your way through life in a way that takes serious ingenuity and intelligence.'

Ares looked at her, eyes glinting, a minuscule smile playing around his mouth. 'That's quite a defence.'

Cassie flushed, embarrassed. 'There was a girl in my school who was constantly sidelined and put at the bottom of the class, just because she had difficulty reading and writing. It made me so mad. Anyone could see she was more intelligent than the rest of us.'

'You pitied her.'

Cassie let out a short sharp laugh at the thought of the only friend she'd really made at boarding school allowing anyone to pity her. 'No way, she pities *me*. She's a force. She's already working at the UN.'

Cassie started walking again, following the flow of tourists to the best vantage point for watching the sunset. She gestured to Ares, who kept pace easily beside her. 'You're one of those success stories.'

His mouth compressed and he said, 'It's more that I was bred to be a success no matter what.'

Cassie thought to herself that she was sure it was more than just breeding, but Ares put his hand on her elbow to steer her through thickening crowds and that made any more words dissolve on her tongue.

They were approaching the promontory now, a vantage point that afforded a ringside view for the setting sun, which was slowly but steadily getting closer and closer to the horizon.

Ares guided Cassie to one of the few spots that hadn't been taken and they sat down, surrounded by chattering tourists, all facing the same way, oohing and ahing as the sky started to go through a veritable kaleidescope of colours.

'You know, you'd be getting just as specatacular a view from your boat and it wouldn't be half as crowded.'

But I'd be lonely. Cassie wondered if she would have had the nerve to come and do this if she'd been on her own. She liked to think so but she hadn't thought twice with Ares. Even if he was here at the behest of her brother and not because he wanted to be. That stung a little.

'Oh, be quiet and enjoy the view,' she said.

Be quiet. Ares had never been told to be quiet by a woman. Or anyone, for that matter. And yet he wasn't insulted. He knew he was grumbling like a petulant teenager. This woman seemed to bring out aspects of him that he'd never encountered before.

And he had never, *ever*, willingly revealed to anyone about his dyslexia. The army had known, and his staff knew but that was because he would never let his dyslexia compromise a security situation. By now he managed it pretty well, but Cassie was right, he'd had to mask it for a long time.

She'd sounded so indignant on his behalf...it had roused something suspiciously expansive in his chest. For a moment he'd imagined what it might have been like to have someone in his corner as a child—helping him navigate a world where letters and numbers had danced in front of him and refused to make sense.

He had to acknowledge uncomfortably that she wasn't at all what he might have expected. She was here, on her own, not just helming her own boat. No staff. No lackeys. Self-sufficient in a way that made him think she must have been on her own a lot as a child.

She was capable. And not looking to see who was looking at her. Ares glanced around briefly, instinctively checking who might be watching them as much as to see if anyone had recognised her. No. She did blend in with the crowd of golden-skinned tourists, watching a sunset. Of course, if anyone chose to really look, they might recognise the pedigree that she carried with a self-assurance that came only with birth. A high-born birth. But even now Ares could imagine her pointing out that she hadn't asked to be born into a royal lineage. And yet she seemed resigned to her fate. To carry on the line. To do her job.

After a few minutes Cassie turned to face him. She'd slid her sunglasses on her head and the brightness of those blue eyes cut right through him.

'Ready to go?'

He just looked at her. She waved a hand in front of his face. 'The sun has set.'

Ares tore his gaze away from her face and looked out over the sea to where the sun had indeed set below the horizon, leaving a lingering haze of orange and pink and yellow flooding the sky. It must have been spectacular but he wouldn't know because he'd been too busy looking at that sunset reflected on Cassie's rapt face.

He was losing it. He stood up. 'Let's get back, then.' He knew he sounded curt. Abrupt. But she rubbed him up the wrong way. *She rubbed you up the right way last night.* Ares gritted his jaw and let Cassie precede him out of the viewing point.

The lingering memory of that spectacular sunset was fast fading and being eclipsed by the way Ares's hand felt on Cassie's elbow and the jolts of electricity running through her every time their bodies collided as Ares herded her through the thronged main street of Oia.

Feeling a need to resist at all costs—this hijacking of her precious freedom, and this assault on her senses—Cassie stopped and dug her heels in. 'I'm hungry. I'd like to eat before going back to the boat.'

Waves of displeasure emanated from Ares. It was almost worth it to rise him. It felt like a dream that they'd shared such an incendiary intimate moment only twenty-four hours ago.

But then he looked down at her as people flowed around them and it came hurtling back. The delicious heat of it. The heart-pounding excitement.

He said, 'Fine, I could eat too. There's a place near here.' He started leading them again, veering off and down a little side street.

Cassie said, 'I thought you hadn't been here before.'

'I never said I hadn't been before, just that I think it's become an over-hyped theme park.'

They were going down wide steps now and emerged into a restaurant that was cut into the side of the caldera, with amazing views out over the sea. A waiter came and greeted Ares effusively, and brought them to a table, set apart from the others on a little point. The best vantage point in the place. Ares pulled out the chair that faced the sea and Cassie found herself being touched by his consideration that she have the view before she realised that he was most likely doing this out of habit, so that there'd be less chance of anyone recognising her.

After all, he was hardly Mr Charm. And yet...there was something seriously compelling about him. Cassie hated herself for it but she wanted to see him unbend. Smile. Relax.

They sat down. The stunning view of the high walls of the caldera with the white-roofed houses and blue trim built along the sides like little toy buildings was exquisitely pretty. But Ares Drakos easily eclipsed even such an amazing view.

Cassie focused on the menu, choosing a salad and a fish main. Ares chose similar and a local wine and they handed the menus back. Cassie tried to take in the view but her gaze kept returning to Ares, who was regarding her steadily.

The setting sun made him seem even darker. More saturnine. It made Cassie itch to provoke. The waiter poured some white wine into their glasses and Cassie lifted her glass. She smiled sunnily. 'To new friends.'

Ares didn't lift his glass in cheers. He took a sip of the wine and said, 'We're not friends.'

A dart of hurt along with irritation at his dogged refusal to bend an inch made Cassie open her eyes wide. 'As I mentioned this morning, I think we've already established we were quite friendly...' she lifted her bare wrist and pretended to look at a watch '...right about this time yesterday evening.'

Ares looked at a point over her shoulder. 'That was a mistake. My fault. You didn't know who I was.'

Cassie said nothing for fear of revealing that even if she had known who he was she might still have climbed him like a tree.

'Can we move on from that?'

He looked at her. 'You brought it up again.'

Cassie rolled her eyes. 'Fine, if *I* promise not to bring it up again can we move on? As it appears that we're destined to spend the next week, at least, together.'

'You sure you don't want to go home sooner?'

Cassie smiled extra sweetly. 'I'm sure. As I said, this is my only chance to enjoy some freedom while I can. Something you take for granted.'

'Are any of us really free though?'

'Spare me the philosophical debate, and yes, some are freer than others. My brother certainly enjoyed his freedom as crown prince, before he became king, after our father died.'

'Or, in his case, *not* his father.'

Cassie's smile slipped as she recalled that brutal bombshell. They'd found out mere hours before it had made international headlines and Caius had had to leave Sadat Sur Mer to avoid the scrum of paparazzi who had descended on the island. Not to mention the shock and ire of the people who had idolised him.

The starters were served, traditional Greek salad with a twist.

'No,' Cassie echoed, 'not his father.'

'What happened to you after your brother left Sadat to escape the press?' Ares popped an olive into his mouth.

Cassie tried not to fixate on those sculpted lips. She shrugged lightly, belying the fear she'd felt in those moments, all alone. Abandoned by her brother. 'I holed up in the palace and had to wait it out, as our advisors and press corps came up with a response, naming me as queen. There was no other alternative.'

She had to acknowledge, 'Caius wanted to stay, to shield me as much as possible, but people were angry. They felt betrayed. He would have caused more headlines staying in Sadat.'

'Overnight you became ruler.'

'More or less…but not officially until the coronation.'

Ares waved a hand. 'That's just a ceremony and paperwork.'

Cassie let out a laugh. 'I think Pierre, my chief advisor, who runs on anxiety and adrenalin, wouldn't quite agree. You're not a royalist?'

Ares took a healthy sip of wine. 'Why would I be?'

'Greece still has a royal family, even if it no longer has any power. You come from a dynasty that probably has traditions and bloodlines dating back as far as theirs does.'

Ares went still on the other side of the table. Cassie sensed it.

He said, 'You're not far wrong. Maybe that's why I'm not a fan of entitled privilege.'

'What happened to you?'

His eyes flashed dark golden for a moment. She was transgressing but she didn't care. He'd hijacked her peace. But then he shrugged and said, 'I didn't care to inherit something I hadn't worked for.'

Cassie was sure there was more to it than that but she just said a little mockingly, 'My, my, you must be dizzy on such high moral ground. No wonder your opinion of me is so low. I don't even have a business to inherit, just a rock of land and and an ancient title.'

He had the grace to look slightly shamed. He said, 'It's not quite the same, I grant you. My lack of love for royalty stems more from an unfortunate incident with a princess from another European royal family.'

Cassie's eyes widened. The waiter put down their main courses. She hadn't even noticed their starters being removed. She came forward and rested an elbow on the table, her chin on her hand. 'Do tell.'

Ares couldn't have looked less inclined to tell, but after spearing a morsel of food from his plate and wiping his mouth with a napkin he said, 'Princess such and such... I was tasked with protecting her as she did one public event in Paris and then proceeded to shop and party like a one-woman hen party.'

'So? That can't have come as a massive surprise. After all, my brother did his best imitation of a one-man stag party. Sometimes with you in tow.'

Ares glared at her. 'Not the same at all.'

Cassie swallowed a piece of delicious fish and smiled. 'Double standards much?'

'Your brother is not spoiled.'

Cassie looked at Ares. 'No, he's not.' And neither was Ares, she was beginning to appreciate.

Ares continued, 'I think we both know he puts up that playboy front as a smokescreen to prevent people getting too close.'

Cassie tried not to show her surprise at Ares's understanding of her brother. It unnerved her. If he saw her brother so clearly, would he see all the way into her where she felt as though no one had ever really seen her? Where she'd had to smile bright enough just to be noticed? To mitigate the tension and toxicity around her?

Her smile certainly didn't work on him except to rile him and the way that left her feeling a little out of control and unsettled made her say, 'Don't change the subject. This princess…'

Ares sat back, wine glass in hand. 'You won't let this go.'

She shook her head. 'Nope.'

'Fine. I went back to my room after a long and particularly tedious day of shopping and socialising to find her naked in my bed.'

Cassie let out a bark of surprised laughter and put her hand over her mouth. When she took it away again she said, 'How did you deal with it…without it…?'

'Ending up all over the papers?'

Cassie nodded, mirth making her mouth twitch again. She could just imagine Ares going volcanic at such a stunt. But she could empathise with the princess. Whoever she was. A dart of something hot and not nice went through her at the thought that it might have worked. But the look on Ares's face was so disgusted it told her all she needed to know. He hadn't accepted her invitation.

'I booked into another room for the night. And she woke up to a new security team the next day.'

Mischievously Cassie said, 'So you're telling me that if I were to—'

'No.' The crack of Ares's voice made Cassie jump a little. He seemed to notice and said a little less curtly, 'You're not getting rid of me that easily and if you try a stunt like that, I'll put you below deck. For your own protection, of course. I'm sure your brother would understand.'

Now he smiled and Cassie scowled. She speared

some more food into her mouth to stop herself from goading him any more.

But now it seemed to be his turn when he asked, 'So what is it exactly that you want to get out of this trip?'

Cassie sat back and pushed her empty plate away and took a sip of wine, wondering if she could possibly divert Ares with the spectacular view of the sky turning lavender and purple behind him as night fell. Stars popping out. But she knew that wouldn't work. He'd barely noticed the sunset earlier.

Eventually she said reluctantly, 'To be honest, I didn't really put a lot of thought into it. It just...suddenly occurred to me, as my advisor was asking me to look at prospective suitors, that I hadn't ever really taken time out for myself...and that, in a couple of weeks, it would no longer be possible. My every moment is scheduled, practically down to toilet breaks. My brother got to have his freedom, I wanted to at least...taste it.'

Ares raised a brow. 'Prospective suitors?'

Cassie nodded wearily. 'A whole file of them.'

'Let me guess, they're all from distinguished royal lines.'

'Of course.'

'And are any of them appealing?'

'Not in the slightest. But...when it comes down to it, I'll have to choose someone. But I won't lie, I'm hoping for something or someone better than those files are offering.'

Ares cocked his head to one side. 'In what way?'

Cassie bit her lip and then said, 'I don't want a marriage in name only…for heirs, like my brother was prepared to settle for. I want real companionship. Respect. At the very least.'

She also wanted passion and something much deeper but she could imagine the horror on Ares's face. Or worse, mockery.

Before he could quiz her on that she asked, 'What about you? Don't you want to marry some day? Have a family?'

He smiled but it was grim. 'No way, not for me.'

'Why? Unhappy childhood?'

He looked a little startled, as if he wasn't used to someone being so direct. He said, 'Something like that. To our parents, we were seen as pawns to fit into the family business at strategic points, either in the running of it—for instance, grooming my brother to inherit the business—or by marrying my sisters off strategically to consolidate power.'

Cassie asked, 'Where were you going to fit in?'

Ares waved a hand. 'Some outpost where they figured I could do no harm with my limited capabilities.'

Cassie snorted, making it clear what she thought about that, and then she observed, 'We really don't come from such different backgrounds. You said "sisters"—how many siblings do you have?'

Ares shifted as if uncomfortable. Tough. He knew practically everything about her. He said, 'Just my older brother and two younger sisters. Both are already married with children.'

'And your brother?'

Ares shook his head. 'Not yet but he's under pressure. He's already CEO and his children will inherit the legacy and carry the name. I was never really interested in the business.'

'How could you have been if you were made to feel it wasn't your destiny?' Cassie observed. Ares said nothing, just looked at her.

Then she divulged, 'If I have children they'll carry my name.'

'That makes sense.'

Cassie's mouth twisted. 'You'd be surprised how many men would have an issue with that.'

'I don't see the issue. Once I walked away from my inheritance my name lost its value.'

'But you started in the army. That's hardly a fortune-making venture.'

Ares looked at her with a clear warning.

Cassie smiled. 'No-go zone.'

He looked at her. 'No-go zone?'

'Caius and I have "no-go zones", when one of us strays too close to something we don't want to discuss.' She leant forward as the waiter gave Ares the bill. 'Are you close to your siblings?'

Something very fleeting crossed his face, and disappeared. 'At one time, maybe, but not now. We haven't been in touch for years.'

It was an enigmatic answer but Cassie didn't push it. She said, 'That's sad. I don't know what I'd do without Caius. I always wished we had more siblings, to take the pressure off just us.' She thought of her twin, and how that might have changed so much. Or perhaps not much at all. They'd never know.

Ares shook his head. 'More siblings doesn't mean less pressure, it's just more opportunities for manipulation.'

Cassie was fascinated by all that Ares was revealing. 'Your parents were manipulative, then?'

He let out a bark of laughter. 'You could say that. But let's get back to what you want to get out of this... moment of freedom.'

No-go zone.

Cassie sighed, looked up and then back and said, 'You won't understand.' He would laugh at her silly wish list. But then, he didn't laugh so maybe he wouldn't.

He said, 'Try me.'

Cassie sighed and divulged, 'OK, I'd like to go to the Uffizi in Florence, during the most packed part of the day; I'd like to go horse-riding on a beach at dawn; I'd like to ride a motorbike along Route 66 in America...but I'd settle for an empty stretch of motorway anywhere really...'

Ares's eyes opened wide. 'You can ride a motorbike?'

Cassie nodded. 'Caius taught me.'

Ares muttered something that sounded like, 'Of course he did.' And then, 'Why the Uffizi on a busy day? When you could get the place shut down just for you?'

Cassie grimaced. 'That's exactly why. I went on a school tour and there were so many daughters of important people in my class that the place was shut down just for us...but I always felt ashamed. It was eerie. I couldn't enjoy the art. I felt like we were stopping people from enjoying it. So I'd like to go back, pay to get in and queue with everyone else…soak up the experience with fellow art lovers.'

Ares had a slightly arrested expression on his face and then he said, 'Is that it? Not an especially extravagant list.'

'I'd like to get a tattoo and go clubbing, proper sweaty-all-night-until-the-sun-comes-up dancing clubbing…'

Now he grimaced, and ignored the bit about clubbing. 'A tattoo? Isn't that a bit of a cliché? Don't tell me, not one of those Mandarin symbols that no one really knows what they mean.'

Cassie vowed there and then to never reveal why she wanted a tattoo. It was way too personal and poignant.

He looked at his watch. 'Is that it? I'm afraid your brother would have my hide if I let you get a tattoo but we could find a club here and by tomorrow be on our way back to Sadat. I'm sure you'll fit the rest of your wish list in over the years.'

Cassie pushed down the pang that he was so eager to be rid of her. It had no place here. That rebellious spark moved through her. She gathered her nerve, sat back and said casually, 'There's something else. I'm a virgin and I really want to have sex before I become queen and have to get married.'

For a second Ares didn't react. His wine glass was at his mouth, he'd just drained it and then suddenly he was sitting up and coughing and spluttering as the wine hit his throat and went down the wrong way.

His reaction helped lessen Cassie's sense of exposure for revealing that. But...he was the one who'd crashed her party and he wasn't going to stop her.

Ares took a gulp of water and glared at her. 'Did you just say...?' He sounded a bit hoarse.

Cassie helpfully provided, 'That I want to lose my virginity? Yes, I did.' She had to laugh at the mix of horror and shock on his face. She winked at him. 'The tattoo probably doesn't look so bad now, does it?'

CHAPTER SIX

IF HE DIDN'T think about what she'd said back at the restaurant, maybe Ares could pretend he'd misheard her. But, from the way she'd been sliding him twinkly blue-eyed glances since they'd left the restaurant and returned to the tender and were now almost at the boat, anchored in the sea, he figured that unfortunately he hadn't misheard.

What he had done was get them out of that restaurant so fast his head had been spinning, as if afraid she was going to go and start propositioning strangers there and then.

As if afraid she'd want to sleep with someone other than you. The incendiary thought crept into his head and Ares mentally snarled at it. He didn't want her. She was too bright and sunny and *royal* and his friend's little sister and totally out of bounds. She was untouched, for crying out loud. He did not touch untouched people. He was too…dark. Cynical.

A man like him and a woman like her did not mix. He would take her brightness and dim it.

But even as he thought of that he almost shook with the enormity of the fact that she was innocent, and what it might be like to be the one to touch her, to rouse her, to make her gasp and moan and plead and clasp around him so tightly that—

'So, I guess no clubbing tonight, then?'

Ares was pulled out of his feverish circling thoughts. The tender was at the boat now, and Cassie was reaching out to grab the ladder that they'd used to climb down from a platform that could be lowered at the back of the boat, while anchored.

'No,' Ares issued through his teeth. He was seriously considering his threat of putting her below deck and keeping her there. But that would mean going down there and even that short visit earlier had been enough to make him sweat. The last thing he wanted was for those far too bright and inquisitive blue eyes to notice. She already saw far too much.

She'd had him spilling about his family, who he never spoke about. And her perceptiveness had surprised him. How she'd put a finger on the fact that he'd never been encouraged to think of the family business as something he could be part of in a meaningful way because his parents had deemed him somehow not useful.

But far more disturbingly he now ached to be the first man to make her moan and clench as she had last night in the bar. If he'd realised then that Caius had spoken the truth and that she really might be innocent... *Theos*. It was too much.

For the first time in a long time, Ares was out of his depth and it was in a way he wasn't prepared for.

Cassie secured the tender to the boat and climbed

the ladder. The night was still and warm. From above him on the boat Cassie said, 'That's cool. I heard Mykonos is the place to go clubbing anyway. Maybe I'll try there...'

For clubbing *and* a lover? Ares wanted to untie the tender again and sail as far away from this boat and woman as he could. But he couldn't. So he climbed up onto the deck. Cassie was standing, with her shoes in her hands, bag slung across her body, hair down and wild around her shoulders. She seemed to glow in the moonlight. It made something inside Ares's chest feel tight and achy.

She said, 'Well, goodnight, then, help yourself to one of the spare cabins.'

'I'll sleep up here.'

Cassie had been turning away and then turned back. She must have seen something on Ares's face because she shrugged and said, 'Whatever.' She turned away again and disappeared down into the belly of the boat. Ares shuddered just thinking about it.

He looked out over the dark mass of the sea. Why did it feel as though what should be the easiest assignment on the planet—babysitting a princess—had just become the most challenging?

The next day, after a light breakfast that Cassie had brought up to the deck to eat, they set off again. Ares had retreated to his taciturn self. He'd disappeared below, presumably to shower and change because he had changed, into board shorts and a T-shirt, but he'd been so quick that Cassie had barely noticed his disappearance as she'd focused on plotting the next stage of the journey.

She turned around and he was back and changed. Only the fact that his hair was damp gave any sign that he'd showered.

His eyes were hidden behind dark shades and his jaw was as hard as ever. Cassie sighed. He was like a formidable piece of rock. And really, she'd not learned much about him last night. She suspected there was a lot more to his break with his family than just a desire to make his own way. No one joined an army to make a fortune. They went into armies to escape something.

'Where are we headed?'

'Mykonos,' she threw over her shoulder. 'It's famous for its clubbing scene. They call it the Ibiza of Greece.'

'Fantastic.'

'Oh, lighten up, you might even enjoy it.'

Cassie smiled to herself. She could feel the way Ares was bristling behind her. Was it wrong that riling him felt so right?

He sat on one of the benches in her peripheral vision, legs spread. She didn't have to look to know his bare legs were as muscled and strong as the rest of him.

When he didn't make any attempt to converse she asked sweetly, 'How was your night on deck?'

'Fine.'

'Is that a security thing? To keep an eye out?'

He huffed and said, 'Something like that.'

Cassie rolled her eyes and shut her mouth. She

needed her wits to navigate through the Cyclades. Mykonos was on the other side of Naxos and Paros, so she focused on that for now and tried to block out the brooding muscled man-mountain sitting far too close for comfort.

When they approached the island, Cassie dropped the anchor in a sheltered spot and busied herself getting the tender into position.

'You're going onto the island now?'

Cassie turned from the small lower deck and looked up. 'Yes, that's my plan.' She smiled sunnily. 'You're welcome to join,' knowing full well he'd have to come with her.

'What's your plan?'

'Well, some lunch to start with, I'm starving, and then shopping. And then, later, clubbing.'

Ares didn't smile. 'Sounds delightful.'

After Cassie had secured the boat, and they were in the tender heading towards the old port, she tried her best not to be so aware of Ares. It annoyed her that he appealed to her so much. He was like a dark cloud. *A dark sexy stormy cloud.* And she hated that she felt the urge to make him smile, look happier. Because that pushed way too many buttons. She'd spent her life trying to make her parents smile and be happier and it hadn't worked.

To know that nothing you'd done had had a positive effect on the people around you in spite of your best efforts was not nice. It was why she'd oftentimes felt invisible. And yet she couldn't join Ares where he was, her inner spirit was just too buoyant no matter how much she might try to deny it.

When they had secured the tender, Ares said, 'Where to now?'

'Mykonos town.'

He hailed a cab and they were being spirited away from the port within minutes. Cassie realised that she hadn't paid for anything yesterday and Ares had just handed the driver some euros.

She said, 'I don't expect you to pay. I'll give you what I owe, and for dinner last night.' He'd all but run her out of the restaurant after she'd told him she planned to lose her virginity. She still couldn't believe she'd had the gall to say that. But it had been worth it for the look of shock on his face.

The fact that he'd populated her dreams last night made it slightly less worth it. Because he was welded to her side for the foreseeable future and so the chances of her actually getting to lose her virginity with anyone seemed to be challenging in the extreme.

Unless you lost it to him, whispered a little voice. As if Cassie didn't already have that incendiary moment from their first night branded onto her brain for ever. Moaning into his mouth as she pushed herself into his hand.

'Are you all right? You've gone very red.'

Cassie saw the town centre approaching and said to the driver in a panic, 'We'll get out here, *efharisto*,' and she all but jumped out of the car as it was still moving in a bid to get away from that dark incisive gaze.

She strode forward into the shopping district and pulled a baseball cap onto her head, praying Ares would leave it alone.

An hour later, as Ares sat on a bench outside a boutique, sipping a small and perfect espresso, he had to acknowledge that he hadn't had this kind of time off in...*ever*, and, while it was disconcerting, it wasn't unenjoyable.

No wonder so many of his peers preferred babysitting royals and celebrities. This was positively civilised. If a bit mind-numbingly boring. Shopping bags were scattered at his feet. And Cassie had just entered the umpteenth boutique.

She'd said a short while before, 'I know you must think this is so typical but, for what it's worth, I never get to just...shop. I'm supplied with clothes by a stylist.'

She'd sounded so defensive and had been looking up at him from under the lip of her baseball cap in a way that had made him want to bend down and capture those plump lips against his, and press against her. So he'd said curtly, 'I'm not thinking anything.'

For a second she'd looked almost stricken but then those bright blue eyes had flashed and she'd said something like, 'Yeah, right, silly of me to assume so.' And she'd disappeared into another shop.

Strange, but Ares had almost felt...guilty. Because the truth was that he *was* assuming and thinking about her. So hard his head hurt. As much as his body. Ever since he'd laid eyes on her. *And your hands*. He gritted his jaw to stop that flood of memories. And he was certainly not imagining her right now, peeling off the knee-length cut-off jeans that hugged her high firm ass like a second skin, or the plaid sleeveless shirt that she'd tied at her waist. Or the plain flat sneakers on her feet and the cute little silver or gold anklet around one impossibly slim ankle.

A bell rang and Ares looked up to find the object of his thoughts standing in front of him holding another shiny bag, smiling. 'Lunch? There's a salad bar nearby.'

Ares stood up and picked up the other bags. 'Lead the way.' Ares knew he was being a grim asshole but the sunnier she was, the grimmer he got, because if he cracked and let one ounce of that sunshiney lightness in, he wasn't sure he wouldn't disintegrate completely.

Just before they reached the restaurant though, a couple emerged, shouting volubly at each other. They were having a fight, the woman gesticulating angrily. They walked away, down the street, still arguing, and Ares moved to let Cassie precede him into the restaurant but she wasn't moving. Or smiling.

He looked at her. Her gaze was fixed on the retreating couple and her eyes were wide. Her face was blanched of all colour. She looked stricken. Or winded, as if someone had just punched her.

An unfamiliar sensation gripped Ares's insides... concern? He reached for her arm and put a hand around it. Not even that shook her out of the trance. He squeezed gently, ignoring the way her arm felt under his hand. 'Cassie?'

Eventually she averted her gaze and looked at him. And blinked. Ares was frowning now. 'Cassie? Do you know those people?'

She blinked again and seemed to come back from a long distance. 'Who?'

Ares jerked his head in the direction of the couple who he could still hear. 'The people having a fight.'

Colour seeped back into Cassie's cheeks and she avoided his eye now. 'No, of course not.' She moved into the restaurant, dislodging his hand from her arm.

They settled into a booth in the restaurant. Ares put Cassie facing the view again, less chance of her being recognised. *And watched by others who could recognise a rare beauty?* He scowled. But his mind was still on that weird little moment outside.

Before he could ask her about it though, she was saying, 'One day the wind will change and your face will stay stuck like that.' She smiled cheekily and then she put a hand to her mouth and took it down and said even more cheekily, 'Oh no, that's what already happened, it's too late!'

She collapsed in a fit of giggles at her own joke and Ares couldn't help it, he felt an alien warmth spreading into his chest and his mouth tugging up and wide. The strange moment was gone. Maybe he'd imagined it? She looked impossibly young and lovely and yet all grown up too. A woman. Who hadn't yet been touched. Not even that reminder could stop her infectious mirth from reaching out and winding around him like a benevolent breeze urging him to just…unbend a little.

She pointed. 'Oh my God! I've done it. I made you crack. And all it took was—' once again she inspected that bare wrist, and looked back at him '—forty-eight hours? Is that a record? Has anyone beaten me?'

'Ha ha,' Ares said, feeling testy but also zingy.

The waiter came and took their orders. When he'd left, Cassie said, 'Lunch is on me, I insist. For that rare smile alone. I mean, I get it, you're in security. It's on brand to look hard and tough and humourless...'

Ares wanted to glare at her but he couldn't quite manage it. Was he really so humourless? He suddenly felt weary. As if he'd been carrying a weight he hadn't even recognised until this moment. He had been humourless for a long time. Since the kidnapping. Since it had become so painfully apparent that his parents couldn't have cared less if he lived or died. Since the chasm had grown between him and his brother and sisters because he couldn't articulate what had happened to him.

Before he could let it go completely he said, 'What was that back there?'

'What was what?' Cassie looked at him, eyes wide and innocent. He didn't trust it for a second.

'You know...the couple arguing and your reaction like you were taking it personally.'

She shook her head. 'Nothing. I just...had a moment. Déjà vu, or something.'

Then, before he could ask any more about it, she grinned and leaned forward. 'Hey, guess what I found?'

Ares tried not to let his gaze drop to the vee in her

shirt where he knew he'd see the swells of her perfect breasts encased in lace. Or maybe nothing. Maybe she wasn't wearing a bra. His body jumped at that and blood rushed to his groin. He shifted.

He indulged her even though he had the definite sense she was distracting him. 'What did you find?'

She sat back, triumphant. 'A tattoo parlour.'

Ares shook his head. 'No way, you're not getting a tattoo, not on my watch.'

Cassie shook out a napkin with a flourish as their salads were delivered. 'I'm afraid to burst your bubble but you can't stop me. I'm a grown woman and you're literally not the boss of me.'

'No, but I am your protector.'

'Well, you can protect the entrance of the parlour while I'm inside. It won't take long. It's not a big tattoo, I promise.'

Ares put his hands up. 'I'm not the one who'll be under the world's lens with everyone debating the meaning of ink on your unblemished skin.'

She cocked her head. 'You think my skin is unblemished?'

Yes, damn her, every toned and golden inch of it. Ares cleared his throat. 'It's not becoming of a queen.'

Cassie speared some cheese and popped it into her mouth, saying, 'Well, it's a good thing I'm not queen yet, isn't it?'

'And did your parents never teach you not to eat and talk at the same time?'

Ares was surprised at the way her face momentarily fell, before she brightened again and swallowed her food before saying, 'No, they were too busy engaging in domestic warfare. But our nannies did their best, if they lasted long. Caius did tend to wear them out.'

Ares picked up on what she'd said and saw the arguing couple in his mind's eye and her reaction to it. 'Domestic warfare?'

Cassie's brightness dropped a few volts again and it was as if the sun disappeared behind a cloud. He hated to admit it but he didn't like it.

She said breezily, 'Forget I said anything, a slip of the tongue.'

To avoid thinking about that tongue and how it had felt tangling with his, Ares said, 'They didn't get on?'

Cassie looked at Ares warily. 'Did Caius ever talk about it?'

He shook his head. No, they hadn't talked about family. Because Caius was in the realm of arranged marriages, or had been, and Ares had no intention of inflicting the Drakos name on children he would inevitably mess up. His own parents hadn't even tried to save him when he'd been in peril and the rest of the time they'd had a series of cold and aloof nannies—how the hell would he know what to do?

In their worlds—his, and Cassie's to a greater extent—children were born to continue legacies or bloodlines. He had no desire to inflict that on a child.

He'd carved out his freedom and on that note he could actually empathise with Cassie. He knew what it felt like to want to break away.

'Well, there's not much to tell, except that…' Cassie stopped and blew some hair out of her face, which only drew Ares's eye to her finely etched jaw and high cheekbone. Those pouty lips.

'Look,' he said, regretting drawing her into this, 'if you don't want to—'

She cut him off. 'They despised each other, that's the truth. They fought all the time. It was like a minefield living with them. They both had affairs. They crucified each other.'

Ares went still. He could see it all too easily. 'That's what happened back there, wasn't it? Your reaction to that couple fighting.'

She shrugged minutely. 'I hate seeing people shouting at each other.'

Ares guessed it was more than that. Her response had been stricken, as if they'd shouted at her.

His parents hadn't actively hated each other but they certainly hadn't *loved*. Not that that even existed.

Cassie went on, 'When my father died in the skiing accident, my mother went on holiday with her latest lover, after pretending to be griefstruck for the cameras of course. And when *she* died a few months later, everyone said wasn't it so romantic, that she obviously hadn't been able to live without him.'

Ares heard the cynicism in Cassie's voice. And something more hollow. Disappointment?

'What had you expected?'

She looked at him with narrowed eyes. 'Was it too much to expect parents who respected each other at least and who showed the minimum of care for me and my brother?'

'No,' Ares said quietly. 'Everyone deserves that.'

With a mocking tone that didn't suit her, Cassie said, 'And some even get more than that, parents who actually love each other and who love their children.'

Ares bizarrely felt like comforting her. He pointed at her. 'Now that is way too much to ask for. That's just an urban myth.'

Cassie smiled but it was small and made Ares miss her full wattage. But wasn't this just proof that being in close proximity to him was only going to dim her light? Something moved through him, a need to restore Cassie's ebullience.

He called for the bill and when Cassie looked at him quizzically, he said, 'Well, if you're going to fit in a tattoo *and* delivering all that shopping back to the boat before going out tonight, we'd better move.'

When her eyes opened wide and she grinned at him Ares fought the counter urge to scowl. The fact that it had unnerved him to hear about her reaction to her parents' marriage and to see her lose her sparkle was far too disturbing to countenance. And why he was encouraging her in her pursuit of this wish list...he really was losing it.

'You're not going to let me see it?'

Cassie shook her head and held her arm against herself. There was a big white plaster over the tattoo that she'd got along the inside of her wrist. 'Not yet anyway. I need to keep it covered for twenty-four hours.'

They'd returned to the boat a while ago and Cassie had taken her shopping down to the cabin. Ares was delaying the moment he would have to go down there and shower and change. He was a coward. He knew it and it sat within him like an acidic little demon.

Cassie had prepared a light dinner of pasta and salad and it was surprisingly delicious. Ares asked, 'Where did you learn to cook?'

'Go on, you can admit it, I'm not what you had me boxed away as on first sight.' She grinned at him and it made his chest feel full.

'You are definitely a novel experience.'

'I was obsessed with cooking shows when I was small. The palace kitchen staff set up a small area for me so I could pretend to cook alongside them. The main cook, a woman called Maria, was probably more of a mother to me than anyone else. She was kind and warm.'

'Sweet story.'

Cassie just grinned even harder at him. 'What about you? Don't they teach you to cook in the army?'

Ares nodded. 'Rudimentary stuff, yes. I can cobble together a meal with whatever is there.'

'Great, then you can do dinner tomorrow night.'

Ares grimaced at the thought of lingering down in that cabin with the boat around him, encroaching on him. Darkness. Cruel hands and fists raining down on him. *He's just some rich kid who no one cares about.*

He swallowed it all down and looked at Cassie. 'That's fair.'

Cassie stood up and gathered the plates. 'I'm going to get ready. See you back up here in an hour?'

Ares nodded. The sun was setting, turning the sky pink and orange and ochre. But already he was dread-ing seeing what concoction Cassie was going to appear in because he knew she could be wearing an oversized sack and he would burn for her.

He smiled mirthlessly to himself. This was torture pure and simple. All of his sins were being called in and there was nothing he could do about it.

Cassie looked at herself in the mirror and her heart thudded too loudly. She'd heard Ares coming down, doing something with dishes in the galley area, and then after a silence he'd gone back up. It was as if he didn't like coming down into the cabin. Sleeping on the deck. She shrugged to herself. Maybe it was an army thing. He certainly hadn't held over anything, like being precious, from his days as an heir to a vast fortune.

She still felt a little raw after that far too revealing episode earlier when she'd reacted to seeing the couple arguing. They'd caught her by surprise, the violence of their words and actions hurtling her back in time before she could steel herself against it. She still had such an immediate visceral response to witnessing confrontations. And Ares had noticed. And put two and two together once she'd let slip about her parents. It had surprised her how easy it had been to reveal that, even if she hadn't revealed the extent of how much it got to her.

She'd sensed an affinity with him, as if he understood something of how it affected her.

She'd plaited her hair and coiled it up onto her head.

She'd put in dark-coloured contact lenses again—just in case. Heavy eye make-up. Glitter across her cheeks.

She was wearing a light blue silk jumpsuit. Sleeveless and with a deep vee, gathered at the waist and at the ankles. Sticky tape holding it in place was preserving her modesty but she knew deep down with an illicit thrill that she didn't much care about preserving her modesty around Ares.

She wanted him. It beat deep within her. Even with all of his grumpy surliness. Today, she'd seen something lighter and that smile. She could still remember it, and how it had transformed his face. It had made her feel pathetically triumphant. But also something else, something more emotional.

No. Not emotion. Desire. She wanted to kiss him again. Feel his hands on her. She wanted him to show her how it could be, so that, no matter what happened, she would have this to treaure inside herself for ever.

She knew she wouldn't even notice another man while he was in the vicinity. He was magnetic. And…a small rogue part of her wondered what it would take to really make him crack open. Lose his control. The thought of being able to have that effect on him was seriously heady.

But doubt crept in. Maybe after that first night her gauche responses had put him off. And now he was here as her reluctant keeper and the last thing he'd want to do was sleep with her. He resented her. She was less worthy than any other client he could have.

And then Cassie shook herself out of it. She *was*

worthy. When Ares looked at her, he really looked at her. She wasn't invisible to him. Except, earlier, when he'd told her he hadn't been thinking or assuming anything about her, that had felt like a knife sliding into tender skin. It had shocked her how much his words could hurt her. He was still little more than a stranger. And yet one who had become central to her existence.

Cassie suddenly felt vulnerable—Ares's opinion meant something to her. She wanted him to like her. Care for her. Respect her. *Want her*. And that was too dangerous. He already had the power to hurt her.

Maybe sleeping with him was not a good idea.

She vowed to try her best to slip away from him tonight. Find another man who could make her want him as she wanted Ares. Surely that wouldn't be so hard? He couldn't have ruined her for other men after little more than a kiss?

Ares wasn't sure how he was managing to command his motor skills because every functioning brain cell had migrated to his pants ever since he'd watched Cassie emerge onto the deck of the boat in a silk jumpsuit that bared her practically from throat to navel.

He'd hardly taken in the coloured lenses in her eyes or the glitter along her cheekbones making them stand out even more. The dark kohl around her eyes. Hair up in a braid and pinned to her head, making her look like a beautiful bohemian art student, exposing her graceful neck and that spectacular bone structure.

They were walking into the beach club now, famous

for its legendary full moon parties that spilled onto the beach. Ares sent silent thanks up that it wasn't a full moon tonight. He felt feral enough as it was.

He steered Cassie over to a roped-off VIP area and ordered drinks. They were looking over the dance floor—heaving with lithe bodies and arms in the air as a world-famous DJ worked his magic at the decks.

When champagne had been delivered, Ares handed her a glass and said, 'Well, is it everything you'd hoped for?'

Cassie was staring around her, taking it all in. Ares hated the lenses dimming those blue eyes but it did make her blend in more.

She nodded. 'Yeah, it's pretty cool.' She looked at him, 'This is nothing new for you—I saw pictures of you coming out of places like this with my brother.'

Ares made a face. 'It was more your brother's scene than mine, to be honest. I'm not a dancer.' Or a charmer, like Caius.

Cassie laughed and it sounded so light and joyful that it had a physical effect, rippling along his nerve ends.

'Believe me, Caius cannot dance.'

Ares gestured with his head towards the dance floor. 'They're not exactly dancing, more like jumping around.'

Cassie rolled her eyes. 'OK, Granddad, I'm going down to dance, or jump around, coming?'

Granddad. Ares swallowed down the urge to put her over his knee for her cheekiness. He'd enjoy it way too much. He shook his head. 'You couldn't pay me to go down there.' And yet he'd pulled her close and danced with her in that bar the other night.

She stood up, long legs even longer in the spindly heeled sandals she'd brought with her in a little backpack from the boat. He watched her walk down onto the dance floor, golden and lithe and beautiful. Graceful. Regal. She was used to people parting to let her aside—he watched as it took her a moment to realise she'd have to push through the crowd and it made him feel something very protective towards her, because she wasn't standing there stamping her foot. She was adapting to being a normal person.

She took such delight in things that he knew most people would have a fit over. Making her own food—sharing it with him, it had to be said—steering the boat. Living with no frills. If he'd thought she wouldn't hack it on her own on a boat, he'd been sorely mistaken. He had to face the uncomfortable fact that even if he weren't here, it wouldn't have dented her enthusiasm for experiencing all of these little *freedoms*.

Finding a man to have sex with for the first time. Hot, acrid rejection at that thought filled Ares. And yet what could he do? He couldn't forbid her to bring a man back to the boat if she so wished. Or to go off with a man and spend the night with him.

Was he prepared to stand outside some door while inside she was laying herself bare for some other faceless, nameless man to touch her and glory in all that stunning innocent sensuality?

No way.

Ares looked down at the dance floor and it took

a second to realise that he'd lost sight of her in the crowd. He kept searching for that distinctive blonde hair. The golden limbs. Glitter. Nothing. He cursed. He was losing his touch. This was the woman who had managed to evade her own security team after all.

Ares stood up and went to find her.

CHAPTER SEVEN

Cassie was having a bad case of the 'déjà vu's. Two guys were standing in front of her and trying to ply her with drinks.

'Come on,' wheedled one. 'They're nice.'

'Look, I'm here with a friend and—' The déjà vu hit even harder when a large shape appeared behind the guys and an arm reached in, a hand wrapping around Cassie's arm. 'There you are.'

Cassie didn't even bother to feign that she was annoyed Ares had sought her out. She said to the guys as she walked away, 'By the way, it's not cool to go after a woman and isolate her in a corner. It's creepy, OK?' They just looked at her, mouths falling agape.

As soon as she'd hit the dance floor, she'd known that there wasn't one man there who could match Ares and then she'd been cornered before she'd realised what was happening.

Ares was dressed in faded jeans and a plain white T-shirt. Messy hair, bearded jaw. He made everyone else look as though they were trying too hard.

He brought her back up to their seats. In spite of

being grateful he'd come to get her, she didn't want him to know that. 'Would you not do that, please?'

Cassie sat down. 'I told you before, I can look after myself.' So much for sneaking off for her very first tryst. She wouldn't get as far as the door.

Ares's expression was dark—surprise surprise. He said, 'Some time I'm going to get you to show me exactly how proficient you are at self-defence.'

Between Cassie's legs throbbed at that ultimatum. At the thought of having Ares on his knees before her. *Making him your king.* Cassie shook her head at that totally audacious image. Wrong on so many levels. She wanted Ares for sex, nothing more.

And if she didn't make it happen now she'd lose her nerve. She picked up her bag. 'I think I'm done here.'

Ares couldn't hide the flash of relief across his face but he looked at his watch. 'It's another five hours until sunrise, are you sure?'

What had she been thinking? The thought of staying until sunrise had been slightly over-optimistic. She said, 'I'm willing to rejig my wish list. I can watch the sunrise from the boat.'

'OK, but, for the record, you're the one who wants to leave.'

Cassie hid a smile. As if Ares with his brooding disapproval weren't cramping her style anyway. But it wasn't him. This wasn't her scene but she knew that now.

They left and Cassie sucked in fresh air. The *thump thump* of the music faded behind them. They picked up the tender at the small pier and headed back to the boat, Cassie swapping out her heels for sneakers. She slipped the lenses out of her eyes and blinked to restore moisture.

As they were heading back out into the sea, Ares tensed and said, 'There's a storm coming in.'

Cassie looked to where he was pointing. Her skin prickled at the gathering clouds. She was suddenly conscious of the breeze picking up. She could handle a storm but it was obviously better not to have to if you could help it. 'That wasn't due to hit until tomorrow. I was planning on heading to a marina to tie up in the morning.'

Ares shook his head, just as the first smattering of faint rain drops hit them. 'No time for that. We'll take the boat somewhere more sheltered now and drop anchor. We'll have to wait it out. Looks like a squall.'

'You mean, I'll take the boat somewhere more sheltered,' Cassie pointed out.

Ares looked at her. 'I never said I couldn't sail. I just don't like boats.'

Cassie had no response for that, but when they reached the boat it was raining in earnest and Ares took control as if he were the skipper. Within minutes they'd secured the tender and Ares was saying authoritatively, 'Get the engine started and I'll pull the anchor up.'

Cassie was professional enough on a boat not to argue. Not in this kind of situation. They worked silently and quickly together, as the wind whipped up and rain battered down. They were soaked but Cassie barely noticed. Too intent on guiding the boat into a small sheltered nearby cove.

She knew enough since she'd been sailing with Caius as a child to understand how quickly storms could come upon you. And how dangerous they could be.

'Here is good. Cut the engine and I'll drop anchor again.'

Cassie did as Ares instructed. It was too much of a revelation to get her head around that he could sail. When the boat was secure she opened the door to the below-deck area and shouted over the wind, 'Come on, we need to get inside.'

Ares hesitated, looking at the opening to the cabin with an indecipherable expression. Cassie said, 'Ares? What are you waiting for? You can't stay on deck, it's too dangerous.'

Finally he moved and she went down into the belly of the boat. He followed her, securing the door behind him. Cassie put on some lights. She realised she was soaked to the skin, her silk jumpsuit plastered to her body.

So was Ares. Soaked. T-shirt practically see-through. She could count the ridges of his six-pack. She could see the dark shadow of his chest hair that went in a line down towards his navel and the top of his jeans. That were also soaked…moulded to his powerful thighs.

Cassie dragged her gaze back up. Ares's hair was wet, stuck to his skull. Water dripping off the ends, that almost reached his shoulders now. He looked like a pirate.

He was looking at her, eyes very dark, hard to read. Jaw clenched. So far so normal. When had he not looked brooding? Earlier…when he'd smiled at lunch. Before taking her to get her tattoo. Absently she glanced down at her arm. The plaster had come off her tattoo but she barely noticed now.

She looked back up and little fires raced over her skin at Ares's look. It was so…primal. 'Ares…' Cassie said. 'You're looking at me as if—'

He abruptly turned around and said gruffly, 'Sorry.'

Cassie moved closer behind him, kicking off her sodden sneakers as she did. Her hair was coming down, and she loosened it out of the plaits so it could dry.

She stood close behind him. He was so much bigger than her. He dominated the space. 'No,' she said, 'I didn't mean it like that… I like you looking at me.'

He shook his head and little droplets of water fell. The boat was rocking from side to side but Cassie hardly noticed. He said, 'No, princess, it was a transgression.'

'Don't call me that.' She knew he was doing that now to put distance between them and it made something surge inside her. Hope. Confidence.

He huffed out something like a laugh. 'Even though it's accurate?'

'Here and now I'm just Cassie. Ares…please.'

With almost palpable reluctance he turned around

and she looked up. His eyes were burning. He shook his head again. 'Cassie…this…is not going to happen.'

She moved closer. 'It already happened the other night, Ares.'

His jaw clenched. 'My fault.'

'I wanted it too. I kissed you.'

'You didn't know who I was.'

'I don't care who you are.' She flushed. 'I mean, I do, but it doesn't matter. Here we're just two people. Adults. Who want the same thing.'

'It's not that simple.'

She moved closer, close enough to touch. She put her hands on his chest, his soaked-through T-shirt. His skin was firm, warm. Pectorals bulging under her palms. 'I think it's the simplest thing in the world. I'm just a woman, Ares, and I've never wanted a man the way I want you.'

'You don't know what you're saying.' Ares brought his hands to her arms as if he was going to push her away. Cassie dug her heels in. She wasn't going anywhere. The air crackled and pulsed between them. Between her legs. Her breasts felt heavy, nipples tight.

'Don't you want me, Ares?' She knew he couldn't deny it. It would be like denying there was a storm lashing the boat and sea outside.

His face was taut now, and his hands tightened on her arms. 'I wanted you the moment I saw you that first night, that's why I didn't tell you who I was when I had a chance. I didn't want you to turn away from me. I've never wanted anyone more.'

Relief flooded her. And sharp desire. 'Take me,

Ares, please.' Cassie wasn't above pleading. If she couldn't have this experience with this man, she knew she'd regret it for the rest of her life.

'Cass...'

'Ares.'

Instead of pushing her away from him, he pulled her inexorably closer until their bodies were touching. He looked down at her, fierce. 'Are you sure you want this?'

'I've never been more sure of anything in my life. Make love to me, Ares.'

'It's not love, Cass.'

Cassie loved the way he said that. *Cass.* She shook her head, body going up in flames, pulse tripping so fast she felt breathless. She lifted her arms and wound them around Ares's neck. 'I don't care what we call it, I just want you, now.'

Ares would have to have been made of iron and stone to resist the woman twining herself around him, pressing those perfect breasts against his chest, rocking her pelvis against his raging hard-on.

Breasts that might as well have been naked the way the soaked material of her jumpsuit clung to them, outlining their high full curves and hard nipples.

She's not just a woman, she's a queen in waiting. She's your friend's little sister. These thoughts that were feverishly running through Ares's head were also being fast drowned out by the clamour of his blood.

On a very deep level, his body was recognising this woman in a way he'd never felt before. *He had to have her. She was his.* He knew if he pushed her away she was stubborn enough to wait out the storm and go straight back to that club. And he wasn't having that. She was his. It beat through him, the most right thing he'd felt in ages.

He took his hands off her arms and settled them around her waist, almost able to span it. That evidence of her femininity made something very carnal move through him.

She lifted her mouth to his and the last of Ares's control snapped. He lowered his head and met her, mouth to mouth, breath to breath and…devoured her like a starving man.

Cassie was clinging onto Ares, any sense of trying to pretend to be nonchalant or cool or confident obliterated. He was kissing her and she was fire and earth and water and air all at once. An amalgam of nerve-endings and atoms and cells all mixing to turn her into one big sensation, throbbing with need as he stoked the flames. Tongue to tongue. He tasted so good. And he felt even better, every rock-hard inch of him, and the part of him that she could feel jerk between them, against the denim of his jeans. Against her belly.

Between her legs felt embarrassingly hot and damp. Was it normal to be so…*wet*? Who cared? One hand was on her waist, gripping her, and the other was in her hair, tangling, tugging her head back so he could take the kiss even deeper.

Cassie wasn't sure how she was standing. The earth

was moving and vaguely she was aware of the storm outside.

When Ares pulled his head back, Cassie opened her eyes. Everything was blurry for a second and she was gasping for breath, heart hammering. Terrified Ares would let oxygen get to his brain and realise this was a bad idea, she said a little shakily, 'Take your top off.'

He looked at her—eyes blurring, cheeks flushed. Hair drying and wild. He smiled and Cassie's heart turned over because this man didn't have a big repertoire of smiles, as she knew well, but she knew she hadn't seen this one, even on that first night.

It was wicked and very sexy. It told her he was committed to this and something inside her eased and melted even more.

He arched a brow. 'Please?'

'Please,' she said. What was wrong with her? It was as if she'd been stripped of everything civil and she'd become the most basic form of a woman wanting to mate with a man.

Ares reached behind him and pulled his damp T-shirt up and over his head and off, dropping it to the floor. Cassie's eyes widened on his broad and muscled chest, with its smattering of dark hair.

'Oh my,' she breathed, hands itching to touch him.

He said, 'Go ahead.'

She looked up for a moment. She must have spoken out loud. She moved closer again and put her palms on his chest, fingers spread out. She felt reverent, as if she were worshipping a god. A Greek god. She might have giggled if she hadn't felt so serious about what she was doing.

His skin was warm, heart thumping under her palms. She moved her hands down and her nails scraped over his nipples, causing him to suck a breath in. She looked up. He shook his head. 'I'm fine, keep going.'

She went back to her task of exploration. Her hands moved down to that tantalising line of dark hair dissecting his flat belly. And then disappearing under the top of his jeans. Her gaze travelled further down to where there was a very obvious bulge against the denim material.

Her mouth watered. Her fingers were on the button. She looked up. 'May I?'

He said, 'Yes, you may.' There was a rough quality to his voice that sent a shudder of longing through her. She popped open the button and then slowly drew the zip down, releasing Ares from his confinement.

Suddenly it was too overwhelming. She took her hands away and stood back saying, 'Can you…?'

He seemed to read her mind and put his hands to his jeans, tugging them down and off, taking his underwear with them. Cassie's avid gaze was glued to Ares's very hard and very big erection. It was beautiful. *He* was beautiful.

'Now you.'

Cassie looked up and gulped. He was six feet plus of raw male beauty. An experienced man. How on earth could she hope to engage his interest? *He's interested,* prompted a dry voice. Maybe for the moment, thought Cassie, but as soon as he realised just how little she knew…

He reached out and trailed a finger along her jaw. 'If you change your mind, Cassie, it's OK.'

Cassie hadn't expected any of this. And she hadn't expected him to be so…*reassuring*. She shook her head. 'No, I want to… I just…no one has ever seen me naked, except for the women at the palace who dress me sometimes and even they…' She trailed off. Even they hadn't seen her fully naked. Exposed.

Ares found one of her hands and picked it up. He interlaced his fingers with hers and led her back through the space to her cabin. Her bed was a tangle of sheets. *Oh God*, would he think she was a spoiled brat? She didn't want him to be reminded now that she was a princess.

As if hearing her thoughts he turned to face her and said, 'Stop thinking.'

'I… OK.'

He put his hands on the shoulders of her jumpsuit and said, 'Is this OK?'

She nodded. Her skin was tingling where his fingers rested and then slowly he pushed the shoulders of the jumpsuit down her arms. She wasn't wearing a bra and the material loosened on her chest, exposing her breasts. She freed her arms.

She could feel her damp skin springing into goosebumps. Her nipples were tingling. She couldn't look at Ares but she heard his indrawn breath and then something like, *Theé mou.*

She glanced up and his gaze was fixated on her breasts. He said reverently, 'You're beautiful.'

Cassie blushed. Then Ares said, 'Turn around.'

She did and he pulled the zip at the back all the way down to the bottom of her back. He tugged gently and the material came down over her hips and fell to the floor. She stepped out of the legs. Now she wore only her underwear. Knickers. Lacy.

Ares gathered her hair and brought it over one shoulder. The ends tickled the upper slopes of her breast. He put his hands on her shoulders and stepped close behind her. She felt his heat and smelled his unique musky scent. Musky and spicy and something more exotic.

He turned her around again and now their bodies were almost touching, nothing between them. His erection pressed against her belly. Cassie moved closer and Ares's eyes flashed.

'Lie down.'

Cassie really wanted him to kiss her again. But she did as he asked, pushing the sheets aside to lie down. He looked at her, that dark golden gaze travelling over every inch of her. She didn't feel embarrassed or exposed now, just hungry.

Ares came down on the bed beside her and Cassie was unaware of the fact that they were in a small cabin on a boat that was being rocked and rolled due to the storm outside.

There was a storm gathering inside her and it grew under Ares's appreciative gaze. He bent his head and answered her silent plea, capturing her mouth with his, fingers tracing her jaw and angling her head so that he could make the kiss deeper.

Cassie explored Ares, wrapping her hand around a bicep and glorying in the strength of him, then up and around his shoulder and neck, fingers funnelling through silky hair, holding his skull.

She touched his chest, and down, fingers trailing over rock-hard abs and that slim waist and then to the potent evidence of his arousal. Instinctively she wrapped a hand around him, revelling in the sensation of all that power and strength under hot silky skin, the way it slipped up and down his shaft with her movement. Suddenly Ares reared back.

Cassie stopped. 'Am I doing something wrong?' Now she felt exposed.

His eyes were glittering and his cheeks were flushed. As flushed as Cassie guessed hers were.

'No, you're not doing anything wrong, but this will be over very fast unless you stop doing that.'

Cassie unpeeled her fingers from Ares's erection. She bit her lip and put her hand on his ass. 'Is this better?'

He huffed a laugh, making his whole face transform. Cassie wanted to make him laugh all the time. It made him look years younger. Less severe. Less... haunted.

Before she could dwell on that little revelation, Ares was squeezing the firm flesh of her breast and rubbing a thumb back and forth across one nipple. Cassie's head fell back and she let a moan come out of her mouth. It felt...exquisite. As if a wire were directly connected from her breast to between her legs.

And then, as if reading her mind, Ares's hot mouth closed over her nipple as he smoothed a hand down over her belly to between her legs. She opened them, tacitly giving him permission, and her insides burst into flame when his fingers delved between the folds of her sex to find the throbbing core of her body.

Cassie opened her eyes as Ares's wicked fingers explored how desperately ready for him she was. He lifted his head from her breast and watched her as he struck up a rhythm, fingers moving inside, massaging her body and then out again. His thumb circled her clitoris and Cassie's hips jerked.

'That's it...' Ares breathed. 'Let yourself go, Cass.'

This man had already given her an orgasm without even penetrating her body and now his fingers were inside, where she'd wanted him that first night, and suddenly a wave of sensation exploded outwards, suffusing Cassie in a haze of pleasure, her muscles clamping against his fingers.

'You're so responsive,' he said with obvious satisfaction, a look of stark hunger on his face.

Cassie was too dazed to do much more than let the waves of pleasure lap through her as Ares disappeared momentarily and then came back, rolling a protective sheath onto his body.

He came back down onto the bed, and pushed Cassie's legs apart. She'd never been more splayed, more exposed...more vulnerable. And yet she felt strong and powerful. Ares knelt between her legs and ran his hands up over her legs, up to the juncture of her body where she was still sensitive.

'OK?'

She nodded, and looked at his erection again. Had it grown? She suddenly felt trepidation that it would—

'It'll fit,' came Ares's amused voice.

Cassie scowled at him and he came down between her legs, nudging them even further apart. 'Don't worry, Cass. You're ready to take me.'

His hair-roughened thighs rubbed against hers, creating delicious friction. Everything about him was so unashamedly *male*, and Cassie had never imagined a man like him would turn her on so much, but right now she felt as if she'd been made just for him. For this moment. Even if it was in a tiny cabin on a rocking boat.

'Please, Ares…'

He came closer and the head of his erection teased the folds around her sex, where she was now aching for more.

'Patience… I'll have to take it slow.'

Cassie felt frustration and she growled, 'I've been riding horses and motorbikes for years, I think I'll be OK.'

Ares's eyes widened and his amused look was back. 'Greedy little thing, aren't you?'

But before she could say another word, he was breaching her entrance and spreading her wide. Cassie watched him as he slowly entered her fully, her body protesting at the invasion but then softening in increments around him. It wasn't painful, so much as uncomfortable. She moved to try and ease it and wasn't prepared for the flutter of pure electricity that shot all the way up to her brain. 'Ooooh...'

'That's it, just breathe, Cass...'

Cass. She melted and Ares went even deeper. She felt impaled, full. She couldn't speak. She could only feel. And then Ares pulled back out and her body didn't want him to go. She gripped his arms. But just as he was almost out, he slid back in again, and so began a slow and leisurely priming of her body to accommodate his.

And then as her body grew more fluid around him, an urgency built, unlike anything Cassie had ever experienced before. Building from her core and tightening inexorably. Brokenly she begged for Ares to do something to relieve this building tension and he bent his head and kissed her, saying, 'Not long now, *agapi mou*...stay with me.'

Their skin was slick. Cassie put her legs around Ares, heels digging into his buttocks, to try and alleviate the tension. He palmed her breast, trapping a nipple between his fingers, pinching.

'Your mouth...' Cassie whispered hoarsely, half deranged with the fire inside her. 'Put your mouth on me.'

Ares obliged, surrounding that taut peak in heat, teeth nipping at her tender flesh and it was that that finally pushed Cassie over the edge and soaring free, higher than she'd ever flown before. Her body wasn't hers any more, it was in the grip of something primal and timeless as she contracted around Ares's body.

Her orgasm was the end of him. He pulled back, trying to hold on, every muscle and sinew taut, but he couldn't do it, he fell too, joining Cassie in her sea of oblivion, bodies welded together, breathing hard. Hearts pounding for long minutes until, finally, the last pulses of pleasure ebbed away and left them at peace.

Ares's return to consciousness was slow. He felt as though he were climbing through a million layers, and then he had the gut-emptying sensation that he'd never find his way out to daylight again. He was aware he was half asleep and starting to panic. An all too familiar sensation. Claustrophobia closing in around him, suffocating him.

He came to with a start, sitting up in a bed, breathing hard, sweating. In an enclosed space. Very dim light coming through the only window. It took him long agonising seconds to place himself. He was in the cabin. On a boat. *Not that boat.* A sliver of relief went through him but not enough.

He looked beside him to see Cassie in a sprawl. Lying on her front, arms out beside her head. Long back. Hair wild, spread out over the pillow. Sheet covering her bottom. Not even that provocative sight could jolt Ares out of the increasing sense of claustrophobia. It was testament to how much he'd wanted her that he'd been distracted enough to make love to her down here at all.

He needed air. Heart pounding, skin clammy, fighting the waves of panic threatening to pull him down into a nightmare, Ares left the cabin.

CHAPTER EIGHT

CASSIE WASN'T SURE what had woken her but she knew before she opened her eyes that she was alone in the bed that took up much of the cabin. She also noticed that the boat was still, only rocking gently. The storm had passed. In more ways than one.

She turned over and cracked open her eyes to see pale daylight. Sheets in a tangle. She smelled *them* in the air, sex. It made her insides clench as she tried to wrap her brain around what had happened.

She was no longer a virgin. She'd never expected sex to be so...all-encompassing. Transcendent. *Amazing*.

She ached all over but pleasurably. Between her legs felt tender and her face got hot as she remembered how frustrated she'd been with Ares's teasing. And then, the exquisite pleasure/pain of him entering her body.

Where was he? There was no sound from outside the cabin. Gingerly, Cassie got up and cracked open the door. The main cabin was empty. The door leading up to the deck was open though.

She caught a glimpse of herself in the mirror in the en suite and groaned. Smeared make-up, glitter on her cheeks. She washed her face quickly and saw Ares's T-shirt on the ground and reached for it, pulling it on. It reached to mid-thigh. She went up the small set of steps and emerged into a cloudless dawn morning. The storm well and truly gone.

Ares was at the stern of the boat, his back to her. Jeans riding low on his hips. He didn't seem to hear her. She went out, feeling suddenly shy after last night. She stopped a couple of feet behind him, near the control panel and wheel. She cleared her throat and saw him flinch. *What?*

Confused now, Cassie went and stood alongside Ares and looked at him. His hair was wild but his face arrested her. It was pale, almost green. Her initial thought was that he was seasick. It wasn't unheard of even after a few days at sea. And it had been stormy. 'Ares…are you OK? Are you ill?'

He looked at her and his eyes were wild. She noticed that he wasn't really looking at her. More like through her. He wasn't seasick. It was something else. A sliver of fear went through Cassie.

She touched Ares's arm and then down until she could take his hand. She tugged him over to the seat on one side of the deck. 'Sit down, Ares.'

He did. As obedient as a little boy. She came down on her haunches in front of him. 'Ares? What's going on?'

His glazed expression didn't change. He shook his head. 'I can't…'

Cassie thought of something and said, 'Wait here.' Even though he didn't look capable of going anywhere.

She went back down into the cabin and hunted around until she found what she was looking for.

She went back up on deck and handed Ares a tumbler glass with a measure of whiskey. 'Drink this.'

He took it but she noticed his hand wasn't steady so she put her hand around his and lifted it to his mouth. He swallowed a drop. Cassie said, 'More.'

He looked at her and for the first time she noticed he saw her and felt heartened. He took some more. Cassie noticed his hand wasn't trembling any more. She came up on the seat beside him.

The sun was coming up, bathing the wide sky in shades of pink. After a few moments, Cassie said as lightly as she could, 'Was it that traumatic?'

Ares looked at her, uncomprehending, and then he got it. She was talking about him taking her virginity. He shook his head and the ghost of a smile touched his mouth. 'No, it's nothing to do with you.'

But had it been as amazing for him as it had been for her? She doubted that.

'Then…what was that?'

He looked at her and threw back the last of the whiskey. She took the empty glass and put it down. She thought he wasn't going to say anything and then eventually he said, 'I was kidnapped, when I was ten. They held me on a boat. Locked in a cabin for two weeks.'

It took a second for this to sink in, and for Cassie to grasp the magnitude and when she did she went cold all over. 'Ares…' she breathed. 'I didn't see anything online…why…?'

It all made horrific sense now, the way he'd always seemed reluctant on the boat, happy to let her navigate. Going down into the cabin as little as possible. *Sleeping on deck.*

'It's not online because my parents had it all but scrubbed from the web. It's still there if you dig for it but they don't like to be reminded of any chink in their armour, any sign of weakness.'

'What happened?'

'The kidnappers, an organised crime gang, asked for a ransom, but my parents refused to pay. My older brother, he was the smart one, they didn't want to risk him being kidnapped if they paid.'

Cassie shook her head. 'Ares, that's so wrong. Did they hurt you?' She couldn't recall seeing any physical scars but then she hadn't been much focused on taking a survey of Ares's body last night. It had been an instrument of pleasure. Not something to scrutinise. She wanted to though, some day. Lay him out on a surface and inspect every inch of him. She pushed that aside.

He let out a short sharp laugh. 'Not physically no, apart from some bruises from rough handling. A bump on my head. Maybe concussion.'

He didn't have to tell her the scars were inside. To this day. She felt guilty. She remembered him trying to persuade her to take a plane.

'Is it just boats or...?'

His mouth compressed. 'Mainly boats... I'm not great in small spaces with locked doors, but it's not as bad.'

Something struck her. The memory of how he'd

taken charge during the storm. 'How did you learn to sail if you hated it so much?'

A flash of pain crossed his face. 'My father. He would not tolerate a son who couldn't sail a boat. He made no allowances for what had happened—he insisted I sail at every opportunity. After all, I belonged to one of the world's biggest shipping dynasties. He saw it as akin to getting back on a horse after being thrown.'

Cassie's mouth fell open in horror. After a moment she said, 'What a monster. Ares, I'm sorry, if I'd had any idea...'

'No one knows how it affected me. Not really.'

Her chest felt tight. 'Your own parents compounded the trauma.'

'They didn't care. It wasn't them that rescued me, it was the police.'

Cassie sucked in a breath. Her parents had been focused on hating each other more than loving her or Caius but she knew they wouldn't have just abandoned them to their fate in a situation like that.

'That's why you broke with them.'

Ares nodded. Cassie sat back and absorbed this. It had been so bad and the abandonment had been so traumatic that not even inheriting a vast dynastic business and fortune had swayed Ares from his vow to break with his parents.

'What about your older brother? Did you ever talk to him about it?'

Ares shook his head. 'He tried to talk to me, but I couldn't articulate what I'd been through. The terror of not knowing what would happen, of knowing there was no escape. My parents didn't encourage me to talk about it with anyone. My brother was being groomed to succeed, my parents pushed us apart, I can see that now.'

'So you had no kind of therapy?'

Now Ares laughed out loud and shook his head. 'No.'

'Maybe if you had you wouldn't still be having panic attacks.'

He looked at her, sharp. 'How do you know what that was?'

'You saw my reaction to that arguing couple yesterday... I've had to learn to manage my anxiety around witnessing any kind of confrontation. I know it's not as traumatic as what happened to you but—'

He put a finger to her mouth and shook his head. 'It's not a competition, Cass. We've both been affected by what happened to us.'

CHAPTER NINE

ARES WAS MOMENTARILY ALONE. Cassie had gone down into the cabin to get them coffee.

He felt hollowed out after his panic attack, but also something else, a sense of calm. He'd never had that reaction in front of anyone before. He could still feel her hand on his arm, cool, then taking his hand, leading him over to the seat. Her compassionate eyes. So blue. Hair wild and tangled around her shoulders. Bare thighs. His T-shirt.

The fact that she knew what he was going through, albeit for a very different reason. He could still recall the way she'd frozen yesterday. Gone pale. Retreated somewhere inside herself.

The sense of being seen and accepted and understood was…as disturbing as it was profound. Throwing him off-centre.

She re-emerged now with cups of coffee and he took one. 'Thanks.' He noticed she'd put on shorts. He'd never been in this situation with a lover before. Because he didn't hang around or encourage them to hang around. And yet, in spite of exposing himself so spectacularly just now, he didn't feel the need to get away from Cassie.

To his relief, he felt something start to eclipse the cold clammy dread as it receded. Awareness. Heat. *Desire.*

Last night...had been amazing enough to distract him from his surroundings. Not even sex would have done that before. But with her... Something uneasy moved through him. *She's different.*

Yes, because she was so out of bounds she might as well be from another planet.

'Last night,' he said and stopped. Not sure what to say.

But Cassie spoke. 'You don't have to say anything.'

'I don't?'

She shook her head, her hair slipping forward to hide her face. 'I'm sure it wasn't what you're...used to.'

Ares huffed a laugh. 'You can say that again.' He absently rubbed his bare chest. He had to acknowledge that it felt as if something had freed up in his chest. Some resident tightness.

Cassie stood up and rounded on him. 'Well, there's no need to be rude about it. I'll dock this boat as soon as I can and you can sign me up with another babysitter, OK?'

It took Ares a moment to compute the hurt on her face. She went to go back down into the cabin and Ares caught her arm. '*Woah!* Wait just a second, where are you going?'

He saw the turmoil on her face and it lanced him right in the gut because he could see that she knew if she went downstairs he would find it hard to follow her. She pulled her arm free. 'That's the problem, there's nowhere to go.'

A moment ago Ares had been thinking that last night couldn't happen again, she was out of bounds and maybe it would be best to just let her dock the boat somewhere and put in a call to have someone else take over, but now that she was saying that, he found it unpalatable. More than unpalatable. Downright impossible.

'Cass, look at me.'

It took her a second but she did, eyes flashing, jaw tight. He took the coffee cup out of her hand and put it down and then took her hands and tugged her towards him until she fell into his lap.

Yes. She belongs here. With me.

'Ares?' She was rigid in his arms, on his lap, where his body was responding to her luscious ass pressed close to his body.

'Cass, last night wasn't what I'm used to...*in a good way.*'

She relaxed into him a little. 'Oh.'

'How do you think I was even able to do that if you hadn't taken all of my attention?'

'There was a storm, we couldn't have stayed on deck... Maybe you were just looking for something to distract you.'

'I tried to resist you, remember?'

Her face went a pretty shade of pink. He saved her. 'You tempted me from the moment I laid eyes on you and judged you to be a spoiled party-girl brat.'

'I'm not a brat.'

'No, you're not.' She wasn't. Ares knew that now. She was genuine and sweet and more self-sufficient than most people he knew. And she was going to be taking on a job that would demand everything of her. For the rest of her life.

'I should be asking you if it was everything you'd hoped.'

She looked at him, suddenly shy. Bit her lip. 'I...' she said. 'It was the most... I never expected it would be so... Is it always like that?'

He shook his head. 'No, but with you...? I think so.'

He moved under her and saw her blush again as she registered what she was sitting on. And then a gleam came into her eye. 'Could we? Now?'

Ares nodded. 'We need protection.'

She jumped up. 'I'll get it.' She disappeared down into the cabin. The thought that he had debauched the future queen he was supposed to be protecting was not something he wanted to dwell on right now. When she came back, he said, 'Take off your shorts.'

She did as Ares stood and pulled off his jeans and sat down again. He reached for her. 'Straddle my lap.'

She did, the T-shirt riding up to the tops of her legs. Ares bit back a groan when she came into contact with his cock. He wouldn't last long.

'Are you sore?'

She shook her head. 'Not too sore.' She looked hungry. Ares pushed her hair over her shoulders and then cupped her face with his hands and kissed her, getting drunk on her sweetness and the way she opened up to him so trustingly.

She wrapped her arms around him and he let her face go to reach under the hem of his T-shirt—it had never looked as good on him—and found soft silky skin. The weight of her perfect breasts, those sharp nipples.

She gasped into his mouth as he rolled them, pinching gently. Then he pushed the T-shirt up, bunching it, and bent his head, to lavish each peak with his tongue and mouth, until Cassie was writhing against him.

He put his hand between them, finding where she was slick and swollen with need. It was all he could do to find the protection, rip it open and roll it onto himself so that he could say, 'Rise up a little.'

She did, bracing her knees on the seat either side of his hips. Ares angled himself so he was nudging her entrance and then he said, 'OK, come back down…'

'Ahhhh.' He let out a hiss of ecstasy as she slowly came down onto his body, encasing him in heat and silk and that exquisite grip of her inner muscles. He held her waist, guiding her movement. She looked at him as if concentrating on a very hard task. It made something move in his chest, so he kissed her again to push it away and focus on the physical.

Up and down she glided on his body and it was more exquisite than Ares had ever known. They fitted together. He could feel Cassie's movements becoming more jerky, faster, as she chased her peak, and Ares held her hips as he thrust up and deep, once, twice…

on the third time she splintered around him with a cry, her body convulsing around his, sending him flying.

The panic and the claustrophobia was gone, banished. Cassie collapsed into him, head buried in his neck. His arms went around her, holding her lightly trembling body in the aftermath.

Even when the tendrils of his dread did come back to him, as sanity and reality returned, it didn't feel as acute. The sharp edges were softened.

A little later they were still at anchor in the sheltered cove where they'd come last night to avoid the storm, eating breakfast/brunch. The sun was up. It was a beautiful cerulean blue-sky day, no hint of the rain and wind from just hours ago.

Cassie had assured Ares a short while before that they would dock the boat as soon as she found the nearest spot for it. She wasn't sure what would happen now, but she knew she couldn't ask Ares to stay on the boat. And she didn't want to continue this trip on a boat with anyone else. The thought was repugnant and she knew there was no way he'd agree to let her continue without security.

A little hesitantly she asked, 'You're not going to... leave me?' She winced inwardly at how that sounded. Needy.

He looked at her. 'Only if you've decided to return to Sadat?'

Cassie shook her head. For the first time since it had become apparent that she would be queen, she resented the constraints on her life. The fact that she had mere days before she'd have to return and start her life of duty. *Without Ares.*

And even though they'd just had the most…transformative night of her life, and delicious morning sex, she wasn't sure where they were now. Ares was used to this. She wasn't.

Hating herself for feeling so insecure, Cassie said, 'What is this now…? What are we…?'

Ares took a sip of coffee and put the cup back on the small table. He looked at her. Thankfully he'd put on a T-shirt that Cassie had brought him. So he wasn't too distracting.

He gestured between them with a finger. *'This?'*

Cassie nodded, squirming. Ares was probably used to sophisticated lovers who didn't need anything spelled out. Well, tough. She raised her chin. 'Yes, *this*.'

Slowly he said, 'We are two adults enjoying a moment of rare chemistry.'

She registered the word *moment*. 'So this isn't… usual?'

He shook his head. 'No, Cass, it's not.'

Something fizzed inside her. It wasn't just her. 'If I had found someone last night to sleep with…to be my first…'

A thunderous expression crossed Ares's face and he reached for her from the other side of the table, pulling her into his lap. 'I wasn't going to let anyone else be the first to touch you.'

Cassie relaxed into Ares's steely strength. She believed him. He wasn't just helping her to tick off her 'last days of freedom' wish list.

He said now, 'I might have tried to deny it but I knew as soon as you told me you were innocent that I wanted to be the one.'

Cassie smiled. 'I'm glad you were. I wanted you to be too.'

A smile tipped up one corner of Ares's mouth. *'Wanted?'*

Cassie bit back a grin. She loved seeing him smile so much. She waved a hand airily and said, 'Oh, yes, I've moved on now. Twice was enough for me.'

Ares's arm tightened around her and his free hand delved under the opening of the robe she'd changed into after her shower to cup her breast. She sucked in a breath.

His smile grew and turned wicked. 'Are you quite sure about that? Not even one more time?'

Breathless now, Cassie said, 'Well, just to be sure, maybe one more time.'

Ares shook his head. 'Not here. Next time, I want to take you on a proper bed, where I can lay you out and explore every inch of you.'

Cassie's insides clenched at the thought of that, and of being able to do that to Ares. To have him spread out for her delectation. 'That sounds nice.'

His expression turned serious. Seriously sexy. 'Oh, it'll be more than nice.'

'This big bed…where would we find it?'

'Spetses.' Ares named another Greek island, in the Saronic chain of islands.

'Spetses,' Cassie repeated.

Ares nodded. 'I have a villa there.'

'That sounds...perfect.' She felt a little giddy at the thought he didn't want to run away from her at the first opportunity. She stood up from Ares's lap, dislodging his hands from her body. 'There's one more thing I want to do here before we hand the boat back.'

He looked up at her and he was so beautiful and wild against this oceanic backdrop that he took her breath away. Cassie undid the robe and let it fall from her naked body. She went and stood at the stern of the boat and glanced back over her shoulder. 'I've never been skinny-dipping before.'

And then she turned and executed a perfect dive off the boat into the clear blue-green waters. When she surfaced it was just in time to see an equally naked Ares poised to join her. He said, 'You're going to kill me before we even see another bed, aren't you?'

Cassie grinned and flicked water up at him and then watched with very feminine appreciation as he also executed a perfect dive into the sea.

Cassie breathed in, taking in her idyllic surroundings. Dusk was bathing everything in a lavender hue, and lavender scented the air as Cassie walked down a path lined by bushes and shrubs and cypress and olive trees.

A sprawling villa lay behind her and the sea glistened at the end of the path. She walked all the way to find steps leading down to a private beach.

She looked at Ares, who had come to stand beside her. 'This is just stunning. How long have you had it?'

'A few years.'

They'd landed on a helipad not far away a short while before in the helicopter that Ares had organised from Mykonos, after docking the boat at a small private marina where it would be picked up by the boat company.

Ares's estate on the Spetses coast was completely secluded and protected by trees and a perimeter fence. He'd shown her a beautiful infinity pool on the other side of the villa set at the end of a series of rolling lawns.

It was utterly quiet and still and it soothed something inside Cassie. The palace on Sadat was beautiful too but it was always busy and full of people. There was no corner that was truly quiet. She hadn't even realised until now how much she appreciated this kind of space and peace.

'Let me show you around the villa.'

He led her back up towards the building with its white walls and terracota-hued slate roof. One end of the villa was two-storey and Cassie could see a room with a balcony that would give views out to the sea. The master bedroom, she presumed.

The rest of the villa seemed to be one-storey and there was a patio on one side.

Ares walked in through open French doors, muslin curtains fluttering gently in the warm breeze. Cassie thought back to the moment earlier that day when she'd been in the sea, the water silky against her naked skin, after Ares had joined her, and how he'd swum under the surface, catching her legs and pulling her down, kissing her under water.

It had been magical. And so had drying off on the deck of the boat, which had inevitably led to more.

Cassie followed Ares into a large airy reception room, with soft couches and low coffee tables laden with hardback photographic books on every subject.

'As you can probably notice, I have more picture books than word books.'

Cassie's heart squeezed as she thought of his dyslexia. She waved a hand. 'Word books are highly overrated.'

Then he showed her a formal dining room, which led into a huge state-of-the-art kitchen where a man in black trousers and black T-shirt was chopping on a marble island.

'Cassie, I'd like you to meet Declan, my chef. He's been kind enough to come and prepare some food for us.'

Cassie shook the man's hand and smiled. 'Nice to meet you.'

'You too.'

They kept going. There was an informal sitting room with a massive-screen TV. Guest suites. A gym. An office.

Upstairs, the master suite was indeed the one with the balcony overlooking the gardens and sea. It was unashamedly masculine, decorated in dark tones with a massive bed. Cassie glimpsed an en suite with a shower open to the elements and a bath as big as a small swimming pool. Two sinks.

As Ares stood beside her on the balcony she asked as casually as she could, 'So do you have many guests here?'

'Only royalty.'

It took Cassie a second to understand his meaning and when she did she looked up at him. 'You mean...'

'Do I have to spell it out?' he asked with a smile.

That smile made Cassie's insides melt. She shook her head. 'I don't think so.'

'Let me show you your room.'

Cassie appreciated his consideration in giving her her own space. She followed him out of his suite and to another, further down the corridor. Ares opened the door, showing her into a sumptuous suite decorated in lighter tones than his. There was a vast bathroom and dressing room, where Cassie was surprised to see a woman hanging up her clothes.

'This is Marta, my housekeeper.'

Cassie shook her hand. The woman said in accented English, 'If you need anything, let me know.'

She left them, closing the bedroom door behind her. Cassie said, 'Marta and Declan...do they stay here too?'

'Marta lives with her husband, my caretaker, on the grounds, in their own smaller villa. Declan lives down in the town with his partner.'

The bed looked very inviting, dressed in cool white cotton.

Ares took her hand and led her over to the French

doors. He opened them and Cassie saw that there was a small terrace outside, with views over the other side of the grounds and sea.

She felt inexplicably emotional for a moment, not even sure where it was stemming from. Swallowing it down, terrified Ares would see something, she said, 'Thank you for bringing me here…and I'm sorry again about the boat. If I'd known—'

He stopped her words by squeezing her hand. She looked up at him. He said, 'I told you, no one knows. Not even my own family.'

'Caius?' Cassie asked.

Ares shook his head. 'We don't go into too much personal stuff.'

Cassie let out a laugh. 'I'm not surprised. I call my brother the clam, he's so secretive.'

Then she thought of something and went a little cold inside. She pulled her hand free. 'Ares, did you just bring me here because it would be easier to keep me protected?'

It was certainly conveniently cut off from everywhere else and Cassie was just realising how adroitly he'd managed to get her to deviate from her plan. But then her conscience struck her. He hadn't faked that panic attack. She believed him about the kidnapping.

A sense of exposure skated over Ares's skin. Cassie wasn't meeting his eye. It would be so easy to say *yes*, that had been his plan, exactly. And it was a good plan to keep her out of the public eye and harm's way. But that hadn't crossed his mind once.

'No,' he said simply, turning his back on the view and resting against the terrace wall to look at her. 'You're free to go, Cass.'

She glanced up at him. 'And what would happen then?'

'I'd get one of my team to shadow you.'

Her hands went to the wall. 'So, you are ready to let me just...go?'

The thought of her leaving sent a visceral response through him. *No way.* 'No, I'm not. But if you wanted to leave, I couldn't go with you. It wouldn't be a good idea for us to stay together because I could no longer be professional.' *Ha!* Ares hadn't been thinking professionally since about five seconds after he'd seen her for the first time.

'Oh,' she said.

'Yes. Oh. I want you, Cass. It's not about me letting you go, it's about whether or not you want to stay and to explore this...heat between us.'

She looked up at him, a smile playing around her mouth, her extremely distracting and provocative mouth. 'That's what it's called—*heat*?'

He reached for her, pulling her into him, relishing the feel of her lithe body and curves pressed against him. She made him feel lighter. *Thée mou*, he would pay for this transgression but not now. Not yet.

'Among other things like lust, chemistry, desire. Take your pick.'

'Yes, I'd like to stay, and I like lust,' she said with a devilish glint in her eye. Ares thought of watching her dive into the sea naked, how she'd looked like a faerie nymph, a mermaid, with her long golden hair and blue eyes and perfect skin.

She might have been innocent but she was a fast learner and she was moving against him now in a way that was fast short-circuiting his brain cells. Obeying some semblance of self-protection from deep down, he forced himself to say, 'You know that this...between us can't go beyond here, out into the world, into our real lives.'

She went still and pulled back, suddenly avoiding his eye. 'Of course, I know that. We both want very different things, and I...do want a marriage that will be as real as I can make it. Caius might have been happy to have a marriage in name only for heirs and appearances and keep someone on the side, but I want more than that.'

She was a romantic. She might deny it but Ares could read between the words. But then he thought of her with some chinless well-bred prince and a red mist coloured his vision. He told himself it was just because he felt possessive of her. He'd been her first lover.

But, no harm to put some space between them. He said, 'I should go to my office and make some calls, check in on things. Let your brother know you're safe.' *And thoroughly debauched.* Ares wouldn't be divulging that. Not if he wanted to keep his head attached to his body. And he wouldn't even blame Caius.

She was still avoiding his eye. She wasn't like the women he was used to. He caught her chin between his fingers and tipped her face up. 'Don't underestimate how much I want you, Cass. We'll have dinner later. Relax for now, make yourself at home.'

He pressed a swift kiss to her mouth and walked away before he changed his mind and his full weakness for her was made brutally apparent. *To her or to you?* asked a mocking voice. Ares ignored it.

Cassie looked at herself in the mirror. She felt different. Did she look different? She peered at her face. She was a little sunburned, there were freckles across her nose, visible even under light make-up. She could imagine Pierre's look of shock to see his pristine princess looking more human. She grinned. She didn't care. She felt reckless. *Free.* Which was ironic, or maybe tragic, considering that she was about to embark on a life of being followed and scrutinised almost every waking moment.

Her grin slipped when she thought of how Ares had made it painfully clear that there was no chance he would be a part of that future. Not that Cassie had imagined for a second that he could be. Even if he wanted to be, the pressure to marry someone *suitable* was immense. And Ares Drakos, even with his upper-class pedigree, didn't have blue blood running through his veins.

Cassie rolled her eyes at herself. Neither did she. It was red, like everyone else's. The only thing that marked her out was the fact that her upper-class family line could be traced back to pre-medieval times and at some point along the way they'd been decreed royal.

She knew what this was with Ares. A moment. A

totally unexpected and amazing moment. She'd hoped for this, but hadn't really believed it might happen. And with someone so...compelling. And interesting. And intriguing. *Stop.*

She focused on checking her reflection again. She was wearing a dress she'd bought in Mykonos in one of the boutiques. White. Silk. Loose and flowy to just below her knee, the kind of thing she'd never be allowed to wear. It was too young, too sexy. Too revealing.

It was sleeveless and backless. A halter-neck design with a deep vee between her breasts. The top of the dress was held in place by a choker-style neck design, pearl buttons.

The waist was nipped with a band of the same material as the dress that met at the back, just above her buttocks, in a pearl clasp, matching the ones at the back of her neck.

She paired the dress with strappy high-heel sandals and a simple pair of pearl earrings and matching bracelet. Jewellery of her mother's that she'd brought with her. She pulled her hair back and up into a rough chignon.

Cassie stepped back and headed for the door. She was going to meet her lover for dinner. *Her lover.* The thought of seeing Ares made her feel bubbly. Effervescent. Light. Who knew that the taciturn man she'd first met would sneak under her skin and change her life so comprehensively? That a smile from him could make her breathless with a sense of victory?

She knew it was dangerous to indulge in this little game they were playing, but she couldn't seem to care enough to stop it. To walk away. This was just a massive tick off her wish list, that was all. *Sex. Losing her virginity.*

Once she landed back on Sadat Sur Mer, her life would not be her own again, and she would have a lifetime to regret the choices she was making right now.

Ares stepped into the living/dining area holding a bottle of champagne and two glasses. But he stopped in his tracks when he saw the figure of the woman standing on the terrace through the open French doors.

She had her back to him. Her bare back, beautifully shaped and making his hands itch to touch. Hair pulled up, drawing attention to that graceful sweep of neck. A choker of material was at her throat, little buttons at the back of her neck. A white dress, falling from her hips in loose, elegant folds.

Legs bare under the dress, high heels.

Ares knew that for the rest of his life, this image would be seared onto his brain.

As if hearing his thoughts she turned around and the front view was even more spellbinding. The dress had a deep vee at the front and he could see the tantalising curves of her breasts. His hand tightened on the bottle of champagne as he forced his legs to move in her direction.

She gestured at the dress. 'I'm probably a little overdressed but I couldn't resist. I'll never get to dress like this at home.'

Ares felt like telling her she could dress like that

for him but he bit it back. She would be dressing for duty and, some day, her husband. He was glad he'd changed into dark trousers and a white shirt, at least.

'You look beautiful.' The words felt horribly inadequate. She was stunning. And she oozed an elegance and sophistication that didn't just come from her breeding and background. They came from her. She'd be elegant in anything. She humbled Ares.

'Thank you.' She ducked her head, some hair falling forward.

Ares poured her a glass of sparkling champagne and one for himself and put the bottle in an ice bucket. He handed her the glass. *'Yamas.'*

She looked up and smiled. *'Santé.'*

They took sips, eyes locked, sparks flying. For someone who'd always taken feeling comfortable around women for granted, Ares felt unaccountably tongue-tied.

Showing her consummate diplomatic skill, she asked, 'Did you get much work done?'

Ares huffed a rough-sounding laugh. 'Really? We're going to talk about work?'

She rolled her eyes. 'I'm interested. How many clients do you have at the moment? Not counting me.'

'I don't consider you a client.'

Her cheeks flushed and she bit her lip. Ares knew he wouldn't make it to dinner if she kept doing that. He reached out and tugged her lip free. 'Stop that. Your mouth is mine to bite.'

She flushed even more. 'So I'm getting a lover and a bodyguard rolled into one? That's a good deal.'

Ares scowled at her and then he spotted something—he'd spotted it before but hadn't had this chance to ask her about it. He reached for her right arm and lifted it up, turning the underside upwards so that he could properly inspect the tattoo she'd had done on the inside of her wrist.

He looked at the letters, only five of them, and read out loud, 'B-e-l-l-e. Belle.' The E ended in the shape of a heart. It was light and delicate. Discreet. Classy, as tattoos went.

He felt Cassie's tension. He looked at her. 'Who's Belle?'

CHAPTER TEN

CASSIE'S HEART WAS thumping and her chest felt tight. Not even Ares's hand on her arm could distract her right now. She should have known this would incite interest but she'd wanted to mark her sister in some way. Brand herself with her presence. Bring her with her on this journey.

Her voice was husky. 'She was my sister. My twin sister. Christabel. Born five minutes after me. She died shortly after birth.'

Ares's hand tightened around her arm for a moment. 'I didn't know.' He let her go and Cassie brought her arm into her belly. 'Not many do, to be honest. They didn't publicise the fact that my mother was pregnant with twins. She was superstitious. She'd had a miscarriage before I—*we*—were born.'

'I'm sorry,' Ares said simply.

Cassie looked at him. 'Thank you. It turns out she was right to be superstitious. It might sound weird but even though we never really met...except for in the womb, I've always felt her presence. As if I'm living a life for both of us. This whole trip...has been in part because I always wonderd if she'd have been more outgoing than me. More brave.'

'You are brave.'

Cassie looked at Ares and swallowed down the lump in her throat.

He asked, 'Would she have been queen?'

'Probably not as I was born first.' Cassie had always felt ridiculously guilty on some level, as if her successful birth had cost her sister's life. 'I always felt as if something or someone was missing. It made sense when I found out that I'd had a twin.'

'When did you find out?'

'I heard staff gossiping when I was around ten, and then I asked Caius.'

'I can't imagine what it must be like to feel like a part of yourself is missing.'

Cassie was surprised that Ares understood even that much. 'It's like a little ache that never goes away. I'm always conscious of her and wondering what she might be doing. We weren't identical.'

At that moment Marta appeared behind Ares and said, 'Dinner is ready.'

Ares turned around. '*Efharisto*, Marta.'

Cassie was glad of the diversion. She always found it emotional to talk about her sister. They followed Marta around to another section of the patio where there was a table set with white linen and china and crystal glasses. Flowers in a vase in the centre. Candles flickering. Cassie knew she couldn't let this scene go to her head—the woman was probably reading more into why Cassie was here with Ares—but it was lovely.

She complimented the housekeeper and the woman beamed.

When they sat down Ares looked at Cassie. The skin of her inner wrist was still tingling from where he'd touched her. He said now, 'You'll make a great queen.'

She looked at him, surprised. 'Why do you say that?' She'd hoped to make a competent queen at least and not let her people down.

'You're a good person and you care about people.'

Cassie couldn't deny the little glow at his assessment of her. But then it dimmed a little. 'I feel very selfish right now.'

'I didn't have a full appreciation of how much your life will be given over to your duties as queen, before I met you. Or how much of your life it's already taken up, just being princess.'

Cassie shrugged. 'It just was, *is*, my life. School was the only time I really had to myself. University. When I was young I would accompany one or both of my parents to events and functions. They'd be doled out between me and Caius. We rarely got to go together because my parents were usually at each other's throats.

'I would have liked to spend more time with Caius,' she admitted wistfully. 'But the abdication forced us apart. I'm ashamed to admit that I blamed him a little, as if it were his fault. When of course it wasn't.'

Ares said, 'Completely understandable. Overnight you were thrust into a position you'd never anticipated. He had his whole life to prepare and then when you needed him most, he had to leave.'

'Thank you,' Cassie said simply, touched by Ares's insight.

She said, 'He'll be there for the coronation—he's insisting on weathering whatever the public and press reaction will be.'

'I'm sure by then it'll have died down and your people will be ready to accept and welcome their new queen.'

Cassie grimaced a little. 'I hope so. I would like to bring the people of Sadat closer, take away some of the fussy protocols. Open up the palace to the public. Be more involved in every part of society on a much more tangible level. Be more of an ambassador for the country to encourage people to come and visit. We're not as glitzy as Monaco, we have to work harder.'

Marta brought starters, delicious morsels of squid cooked with tomato and basil, washed down with local white wine. For a few minutes they ate contentedly— Ares was easy company.

When Marta cleared the plates away, Cassie sat back. 'So where are your family?'

Ares gave her a look—no-go zone—and she just arched a brow. 'It's a simple question.'

Ares sighed. 'Mainly Athens, that's where the head office is, but there are offices all over the world. Drakos Solutions is one of the biggest shipping and logistics companies in the world.'

'It's the biggest, according to the Internet. You don't regret turning your back?'

Ares made a face. 'I guess I'd be lying if I said I don't look them up, keep tabs on them. The company... *and* my siblings. Not my parents.'

Cassie was silent while Marta returned with the mains, seafood ravioli. When she was gone Ares said with almost palpable reluctance, 'I have nieces and nephews.'

Cassie's mouth opened. And shut again under his look. He probably hadn't intended divulging that much. Risking his censure, Cassie said quickly, 'Well, for what it's worth, they're missing out on a pretty cool uncle.'

Ares made a non-committal noise. Cassie could see Ares with kids. He'd be good with them. Knowing that she shouldn't push but not able to stop herself, she said, 'You could just...reach out. It wasn't your siblings' fault what happened. It sounds like your brother cared to know what had happened?'

Ares sighed and ran a hand through his hair, messing it up sexily. Cassie fought to stay focused.

He said, 'It has eaten away at me, the guilt of pushing them away. Losing contact. My brother is busy, he's now CEO of the company. My sisters...they have their families. The gulf has grown and it's my fault.'

Cassie offered, 'It's on them too but it's easy to let

distance grow. Especially if they think they might be rejected.'

Knowing she was straying way into the no-go zone, she couldn't help asking, 'You really don't ever intend to have a family?'

This time Ares gave her an explicit look and said, 'Your food is getting cold.'

Cassie smiled and obediently took a piece of ravioli. It was delicious. When she thought Ares was going to ignore her question, he sat back and said, 'Why would I have kids when I have no idea how to parent them?'

Cassie put her head on one side. 'I could have the same attitude but I know that I want to do things differently. I don't want my children growing up in a domestic war zone and I want them to know they're loved, and...*seen*.'

'You didn't feel seen?'

Cassie shook her head. 'Caius was the focus, the heir. I think my father saw me like an ornament. He didn't know how to relate to me. My mother was too busy hating him and having affairs. As I got older I think she looked at me and saw herself ageing.

'When they were really going for it, during one of their many arguments, I'd do everything to try and distract them. Be as bright and happy as possible...'

Ares shook his head. 'It didn't work because they were so selfish they couldn't appreciate what was in front of them.'

That caught Cassie right in the heart where she'd

always had that sense of being on the other side of a glass wall, unable to make anyone hear her, or see her.

'*Theos*, Cassie. Come here.' Ares took her hand and tugged her out of her seat and pulled her into his lap. Her silky dress was a flimsy barrier between her and the steely heat and strength of his body.

She looked down at him, heart tripping. His hand was on her bare back. 'No wonder you blasted me with your sunshine when we met. It's your defence and offence mechanism.'

Cassie scowled but inside she was turning into mush at his far too accurate assessment. 'What can I say? Your snark gave me permission to display my true self.'

Ares looked serious. 'I was afraid I'd dim your brightness.'

Cassie's heart skipped about a million beats. She shook her head. 'No, you couldn't do that.' He'd given her something far more precious. A sense of who she really was.

Ares said then, 'There's another reason I never intended to have a family. I don't want to pass my dyslexia on to a child.'

Cassie wanted to reach out and punish his parents for being so awful and cold. 'Even if you did, it's not an affliction, it's just a different way of learning. I think it's an asset.'

'Anyway, it's not something I'll have to consider. My brother will have kids.'

Cassie felt like pushing back at Ares's certainty he

wouldn't be complicating his life with a family but then she thought of him with someone who might have the power to change his mind and make him want things he'd never considered before. A cold weight lodged in her gut, because she was realising that *she* wanted to be the one who could change his mind.

The curse of every woman everywhere who had been told in no uncertain terms by a man that they were not interested in commitment but who fooled themselves into thinking they could be different. Or, worse, *the one*.

Cassie assured herself desperately that Ares had been her first lover, that was all, it was normal to feel emotions attached with sex. It had been a pretty profound experience.

Ares was not someone who wanted to step into a lifelong role of duty by a woman's side. Where he would be required to sire children to further the Mansur royal line. He was a lone wolf. And this was just a brief moment. And the fact that she was even thinking of him in those terms made Cassie lever herself off Ares's lap and back to her seat, forking some ravioli into her mouth before she could say anything else.

Ares just looked at her, as if he had her measure, but she really really hoped he couldn't see into her head because if he did he'd be running so fast in the opposite direction she'd have whiplash.

Cassie woke the next morning to a warm breeze over her bare skin and the scent of sea and pine and lavender. Scents that reminded her of home, but she knew she wasn't in the palace.

For one thing, she didn't sleep naked. And for another, she wasn't used to waking feeling achy but satisfied on a bone-deep level. *A soul level.* She let her mind skitter away from that far too revealing revelation. There was a much earthier smell, the smell of sex. She focused on that and smiled.

'Do you ever *not* smile?'

Cassie's eyes flew open and she was looking at an expanse of toned ridged belly muscles above the line of sweatpants. She dragged her gaze up to where Ares was sitting on the side of the bed.

Cassie's face got hot. Last night she'd lived out her fantasy of having Ares spread out for her very thorough investigation.

'Kalimera,' Ares said, with a very wicked glint in his eye, as if he too was remembering how she'd let him do the same to her, exploring every dip and curve of her body until she'd been begging him for mercy.

'Bonne matin,' she said, using her own language. A hybrid of French, Spanish and Italian.

He swatted her bottom under the sheet and stood up. 'Come on, I've got plans for you this morning.'

'Plans? What are they again?' Cassie rolled over onto her back. She could see that it was still early outside, just after dawn.

When she looked at Ares his gaze was fixed south of her face on her bare breasts. She revelled in his hot look. 'Are these plans…urgent?'

He came down on the bed again and put two hands either side of her, coming down close to her chest. She could smell his freshly washed skin and smiled wider. She'd realised that it cost her nothing to smile and be happy with Ares. It came from an easy place. Not needing to force it. 'I've just added something to my wish list—I want to shower with my lover.'

Ares's eyes flared. He stood up again and caught her hands, pulling her up. 'What a good idea.'

She was in his arms and he was carrying her into his en suite before she could take another breath. She'd never get enough of this evidence of Ares's sheer strength.

He put her down but kept an arm around her as he turned on the spray. Then he pulled down his sweatpants and brought them both under the steaming hot water. He set about soaping up Cassie's body, hands running over her with the same thoroughness he'd used last night. Standing behind her, cupping her breasts and then reaching down with his hand to slide his fingers between her legs where she was already ready, and, by now, wide awake.

He moved his fingers in and out, bringing Cassie to the brink of orgasm, and then he disappeared, saying, 'One second...'

Cassie whimpered a little, and turned around, resting against the wall, to see Ares return, rolling a protective sheath onto his hard erection. He stepped back under the spray and lifted her up. 'Put your legs around me.'

She did, and then gasped when he took her with one deep thrust. It was fast and furious, Cassie climaxing around Ares's body, clinging to him as he found his own release, a guttural groan coming out of his mouth as his body jerked against her, and he dropped his head into her neck.

Cassie felt unaccountably tender, spearing his hair with her fingers and holding him as their breathing came back to normal and the spray fell around them.

A little later, Cassie stopped in her tracks when she saw what was waiting for them outside the front of the villa. Her mouth dropped open as she looked from where the two motorcycles were parked to Ares.

'Ares?'

He smiled a little ruefully. 'I know the coast road of Spetses isn't Route 66 but it'll have to do.'

She couldn't believe it. Emotion surged. She couldn't remember the last time someone had done something so thoughtful. She tried to hide how touched she was, gesturing to her clothes, jeans, a T-shirt and sneakers. 'Now I know why there was a strict dress code.'

Ares was similarly attired. He held out a lightweight leather jacket. 'The bike shop sent this over too.'

Cassie pulled it on. Even though it was warm, she knew the leather would be protective and regulate the heat. She zipped it up.

Ares put on his leather jacket and instantly looked like a rock star. He showed Cassie her bike but she was familiar with the model. She got onto the bike, settling into the seat. Ares came over with a helmet in his hands and looked at her, shaking his head a little. 'I must be crazy to let you do this.'

Cassie took the helmet out of his hands, putting it onto her head. She grinned at him and turned the bike on, feeling the powerful throttle. 'Too late now.'

Ares's jaw clenched but he put on his own helmet and got onto his bike, then he said over the sound of the two engines, 'This isn't a race, Cass, follow me.'

Cassie bit back her smile. 'Aye, aye, sir.'

They set off from the villa and Cassie dutifully followed Ares as he made his way to the main coastal road that encircled the island. Ares drove fast but he was safe. Cassie liked that he obviously didn't feel the need to show off. He was confident enough not to. It was very sexy. And she was happy to stay in his slipstream. She guessed he was giving her time to take in the scenery. After about thirty minutes, when she figured they must be halfway around the small island, Ares slowed down and indicated left.

He turned off the road and went down a dirt track. Cassie saw the sea sparkling in the distance, olive trees lining the track until they emerged onto the edge of a secluded sandy beach. Not just secluded. Totally empty.

Ares stopped his bike and got off. Cassie pulled up beside him and cut off her engine. It was blissfully quiet, just the sounds of the waves breaking on the shore and insects in the undergrowth.

Ares took off his helmet and then came over to her, lifting hers off. She shook her hair out and unzipped the jacket. She could get far too used to this attention and consideration as Ares helped her off the bike.

Her legs were a little wobbly from the adrenalin. The sea had never looked so inviting.

Ares said, 'I found this not long after I bought the villa. It's usually very private here.'

She noticed then that there were two saddlebags attached to his bike and he opened them now, taking out an array of items. Swimwear, towels, and she could see what looked like a packed lunch. A bottle of wine in a cooler.

Ares carried everything down to a shaded spot. He glanced at Cassie. 'I took the liberty of packing for you.'

Cassie raised a brow. 'Did you now?'

He grinned and handed her a white string bikini. His grin distracted her from pointing out that he could have chosen the white one-piece she'd also bought in Mykonos. She took a towel too, and used it to change into the bikini. When she was dressed she jogged towards the water, not able to resist the lure.

She turned back to face Ares, jogging backwards, and almost tripped over her feet when she saw him pulling up a black pair of swim shorts that hugged his muscular physique and left little to the imagination. Not that she needed any help picturing what he looked like naked.

He jogged towards her, easily catching up, and she

saw the mischievous glint in his eye and put out her hands. 'Ares...don't you even dare to—' but it was too late. Before she knew what was happening, the world was upended when he threw her over his shoulder and brought her into the water, ignoring her squeals and protests, dunking them both beneath the foaming waves.

When Cassie surfaced, gasping and blinking seawater from her eyes, she felt so full of gratitude for Ares giving her this experience that she wrapped her arms around him and kissed him before he could see the emotions that were bubbling ever closer to the surface with every passing minute.

Later that day when the intense heat had gone out of the sun, belly full and skin sandblasted and sunblasted, Ares sat by Cassie, knees drawn up. She'd fallen asleep under the shade and his avid gaze tracked over her golden curves. Her hair was spread out, wild and tangled from the sea. Blonde streaks highlighted in the sun.

She'd been so delighted with the bike, and then the impromptu picnic. It had been rustic and basic, but she'd fallen on it like someone who'd just been handed a ten-course tasting menu in one of the world's top restaurants.

The fact that she would be at home in either scenario was not something Ares had ever expected when he'd seen her that first night on the dance floor in the tacky bar.

She'd admitted to him that she'd felt out of her depth and lonely that night. Then she'd asked, 'Are you really here with me because you want to be?' His insides had seized at the thought that she suspected he was only with her out of a sense of responsibility. She truly had no idea of the depth of his desire for her. A desire that wasn't waning. It was growing.

He'd pushed that disconcerting thought aside and said, 'If I didn't want to be with you, Cass, I'd have handed you over to one of my team days ago. I've never wanted a woman the way I want you.'

Ares would never usually be so honest with a lover but Cassie knew where they stood. They were both on very different trajectories. This was just a…moment.

He knew he was playing with fire indulging in this rare chemistry with her. She'd been innocent. She'd had a pretty sheltered upbringing. She might be displaying her sense of insecurity, but he had an uneasy suspicion that it wasn't her he should be worried about protecting, it was himself.

As if hearing his thoughts she stirred and cracked open one eye and smiled. He knew now which smiles were genuine, and which ones were the ones she pulled up out of habit, to project that sunny nature. To defend and protect herself.

In a bid to try and regain a sense of control, Ares came down over Cassie on his two hands and bent his head to hers, hovering over her mouth for a moment, prolonging the delicious feeling of anticipation, and then she wound her arms around his neck and pressed her mouth to his and Ares fell headlong into the kiss, pushing aside all niggles and reservations and a growing uneasy feeling that he'd lost control a long time ago.

The next day...

'Go on, hit me, show me your moves.'

Cassie smiled sweetly at Ares as she moved around him on nimble feet. 'You think I can't take you?'

Ares let out a huff of laughter. 'Oh, don't worry, I've learned that you are not to be underestimated.'

Cassie's smile got sweeter and then she aimed a few jabs at Ares's midriff area and when he looked down she pushed her palm up to connect with his chin. If any force had been behind it his head would have snapped back.

He looked at her. 'Not bad.'

Cassie—still moving—gave a modest shrug. They were in the gym of the villa, and Ares had put mats down on the ground. After a leisurely breakfast he'd said, 'Get your workout gear on—now's as good a time as any to prove to me you could have taken care of yourself with those guys.

'OK,' Ares said now, walking her back towards a corner of the room, 'say I've got you boxed in like those guys had in the bar. What do you do?'

He crowded her, putting his hands up over her head, caging her in. Cassie wanted to scowl. He had an unfair advantage of being far too distracting in a sleeveless T-shirt and shorts. All she could see were muscles.

'What if I told you I'm a lover, not a fighter?' she said, hoping to divert him. Not because she couldn't take him but because she'd prefer to lick his muscles than pummel them.

'Nope. Not going to work.'

Cassie rolled her eyes and as quick as lightning ducked out under Ares's arm and was standing behind him tapping him on the shoulder. He sighed and turned around, and Cassie lifted a knee as if to aim a kick at Ares's groin area but he caught her leg. Cassie twisted to dislodge his hold and feinted away.

She went back into the centre of the room and Ares came towards her, not smiling. It reminded her of how he'd been and how different he was now. It was enough to distract her so she wasn't ready when he quickly sidestepped her and caught her in a choke-hold against his chest, a strong arm across her neck.

She wriggled her behind against a strategic part of his anatomy and when he relaxed infinitesimally, she aimed a sharp elbow at his ribs and used his arm as leverage to get free, while hooking her foot behind one of his legs to send him sprawling to the ground.

Instantly she was down beside him, concerned. 'Ares? Are you OK? To be honest I didn't even think I'd be able to budge you.'

He looked up at her and then, capitalising on *her* distraction, executed a move that had her under him in seconds. He commented, 'You little minx, you knew exactly what you were doing distracting me.'

She grinned, relishing his weight on her. He came down even closer and she wrapped her arms around him.

He said, 'I don't need to worry about you, do I?'

Cassie was torn. After years of her feeling like an object to be moved around, Ares was the first person—after her brother—who really looked at her. Saw her. Was it so bad to want to be worried about? Because that meant someone cared.

But she swallowed that down and said, 'No, I guess you don't.'

He lowered his head and covered her mouth with his and it was only a discreet coughing that became forceful enough to notice that had reality intruding and Ares lifting his head.

He looked up and Cassie's face flamed when she followed his gaze and realised it was Declan and he was saying, 'Sorry to intrude, boss, but your phone kept ringing and apparently it's urgent.'

Ares levered himself up from Cassie and she put a hand over her face to try and hide. But Declan was gone and Ares was on the phone saying, 'Caius?'

Immediately Cassie got up in a fluid motion. Ares was looking at her and saying, 'Yes, she's here. Hang on.'

He handed her the phone and he was grim. Cassie's insides turned over. 'Caius? What's wrong? Are you OK?'

Her brother's voice on the other end of the line said, 'I'm fine, Cass, it's not me. But I think you need to get back to Sadat. Your absence has been noted and speculation is building as to where you are. Some are even saying you don't want to be queen.'

Cassie gasped. 'That's not true. I'd never let them down.'

'I know, Cass, but you should probably get back and calm things down.' After a beat he said, 'I'm sorry you didn't have longer.'

Cassie was looking at Ares, who was watching her. Suddenly it was overwhelming to think that life was rushing back at her. And that this was it. Emotion rose, swift and sharp. Tears pricked her eyes, she turned away and terminated the conversation with her brother and gathered herself before facing Ares again.

He spoke before she did. 'You have to get back to Sadat.'

She nodded and handed back his phone. 'I should have figured that my absence would cause some confusion.'

Ares came close and touched her jaw. 'It wasn't too much to ask to have some time to yourself, Cass. You'll be able to carve out time again—you're resourceful.'

She shrugged minutely and struggled to muster up a smile. She felt flat. Cold inside, because it would be time without Ares. 'I should start packing.'

'I'll arrange your transport.'

Cassie felt that like a physical blow. He probably couldn't wait to be free again. She also suddenly realised there was still so much she didn't know about him. Abruptly she asked, 'Where do you even live?'

Ares blinked. 'You want to know where I live?'

Cassie felt foolish now. 'I just…realised I didn't

know that about you.' Maybe she didn't know because he didn't want her to know.

But he answered, 'New York, mainly. But I have this place here, an apartment in Athens and a place in London, too.'

'Oh.'

'Cass…?'

She shook her head. 'Sorry, I just…wasn't expecting this to end…like this.'

CHAPTER ELEVEN

Cassie's words hung in the air between them. She looked as if the wind had been knocked out of her. Deflated. Ares was numb. He recognised shock. He had to admit he too felt a little blindsided after Caius's wake-up call. It had been all too easy to pretend there wasn't a real world waiting for them to return. Ares to his security business and Cassie to become queen.

What Ares didn't tell Cassie was that when he'd heard Caius's voice on the phone he'd had an urge to cut the connection and say nothing. Because he'd known before his friend had even spoken that this... was over.

But it was for the best. This little...*moment* had been an indulgence Ares should never have allowed to happen. It had been weak. Selfish. He'd broken all of his own rules to not let anyone get close enough to hurt him the way his family had done with their callous disregard. He amended that now. Not his *family*. His parents. His siblings...he'd never given them a chance really and he was only fully recognising that fact after all this time.

Cassie with her questions had made him acknowledge that they'd been pawns as much as he had. It wasn't as if they'd had any power to help him when he'd been kidnapped. And yet he'd cut them off, excised them from his world. One of the tenets of his life, the thing he'd built so much around—not needing anyone, being a loner—no longer felt so solid. *Or attractive.*

His very justified sense of injury was no longer so justified and the woman in front of him, who he'd been moments away from taking here on the floor of the gym like a feral youth, was the cause of this introspection.

Ares didn't need introspection. His life had been perfectly fine. And the fact that her usual sunniness was dimmed…shouldn't matter a whit. He took a step back and tried not to let his eyes travel down over that perfectly honed body, encased in clinging Lycra. Her little midriff-baring vest top and the leggings that cupped her ass like a second skin.

And he definitely couldn't think about the surprising strength that had caught him off guard. But then, that just summed up his whole experience with her. Surprising at every turn.

His voice sounded gruff. 'You should get ready, Cass.'

'Yes. I should.'

Ares mentally pleaded with her to smile, light up again, but she just turned and walked out of the room looking dejected and he had to push down the surge of protectiveness he felt at the thought of her facing everything ahead of her alone.

She wasn't his. And she wouldn't be alone for long. She'd find a husband and carve out a better existence than she'd seen from her parents. He knew she would.

A short time later they were at the same private airfield in Athens where, just days ago, Cassie had evaded her security team and headed off on a solo adventure. Everything felt different though. She was different. She felt as if a layer of herself had been sloughed away and a new layer of skin had formed. She felt more sober. Less inclined to smile for the sake of it.

She also felt heartbroken and she wanted to hate Ares for making her fall for him. But she couldn't. The thought of going back to Sadat and becoming queen wasn't daunting. What was daunting was the fact that she had to do it without Ares, and that he wouldn't be by her side. Ever again.

She was standing in a small vestibule now, eyes hidden behind sunglasses, as Ares spoke to officials to arrange her flight home. This was it. This was where he was going to say goodbye and then it would be as if these last few magical days had never happened—

'OK, let's go.' Ares had taken her arm and was leading her out of the small room onto the tarmac and walking towards the sleek jet.

Cassie tried to get her brain to catch up with her mouth. 'Where are you going?'

He glanced down. 'With you.'

Cassie's heart skipped a beat. 'What do you mean? Aren't you staying here? Or heading back to America?'

'I will be, but not just yet. We're making one stop before I let you go back to Sadat.' They were climbing the steps to the plane now. An air steward was waiting for them, smiling. Cassie smiled back and it slipped off her face as soon as they were in the plush cabin.

'Ares...?'

He was walking through the cabin checking the space and turned around. He was wearing jeans and a dark shirt, sleeves rolled up, buttons undone revealing the top of his powerful chest.

He looked over Cassie's head to the steward. 'OK, we're good to go.'

Cassie folded her arms and cocked one hip to the side, eyes narrowed on Ares. 'Want to tell *me* what's going on?'

He reached for her and tugged her to a seat. He took the one opposite and as the plane started to move he said, 'Buckle up.'

'Not until you tell me where we're going.'

He looked at her and then reached across the divide and slotted her safety belt together. Cassie tried swatting his hands away but the sensation of his hands near her belly and legs made her clumsy.

She was tempted to undo her belt to have him do it up again but resisted the childish urge. Eventually under her death glare, as the plane gathered speed and lifted into the air, Ares said, 'We're making a little stop en route to Sadat.'

'I've gathered that much,' Cassie said dryly. 'Where exactly?'

'Florence.'

'Florence,' she echoed, struggling to understand.

Ares looked at his watch. 'Yes, it's a little over two hours.'

And then it hit her. Florence. Her insides turned to jelly. 'Are we going to the Uffizi gallery?'

Ares nodded. He said a little gruffly, 'I wanted to give you one more experience from your list.'

Cassie shook her head, overcome. 'Ares…' She undid her belt and launched herself out of her seat and into Ares's lap. His arms went around her and he commented, 'I don't think we're technically cruising yet, so you're in breach of safety procedure.'

Cassie knew that if the plane went down in that moment, as long as she was in Ares's arms, she wouldn't care. She felt like crying but she pushed it down and grinned at Ares and wriggled a little on his lap. 'I've got a new addition to the list.'

His eyes turned molten. 'I'm sure we can accommodate late additions to the list.'

A short time later, when they were safely cruising, Ares made good on fulfilling Cassie's wish list. They were in the bedroom at the back of the plane and Cassie was biting down on her hand to avoid screaming out loud.

Ares's head was between her legs, his hands holding her thighs apart, and his tongue was engaged in sending her spiralling into a paroxysm of pleasure so intense it was almost painful. She had her other hand on his head, fingers tangled in his thick hair, simultaneously pulling him closer and pushing him away.

When Ares finally lifted his mouth from her clasping body, he was smiling. He moved up her body, stopping to press kisses to her belly and then enclosing a nipple in his hot mouth, teasing the sharp point with his teeth.

He lifted his head. 'You've now been inititated into the mile high club.'

Cassie was still reeling from the intensity of the orgasm. A short sharp dart of jealousy struck her to think that this wasn't Ares's initiation into the club. But then this was the last time they'd— She reached for him to stop her mind going down that path.

'Kiss me, Ares.'

He obliged, with a deep explicit kiss. Cassie spread her legs wider and reached down, wrapping her hand around him, stroking his erection, making him stop the kiss and hiss. His cheeks were flushed. 'Cass... you're killing me.'

'I want you inside me. Now.' She sounded so bossy. He'd turned her into someone greedy.

He found protection and rolled it onto his length. Cassie already felt the pain of regret and separation and as he entered her, it tinged this lovemaking with an unbearable sense of poignancy. This time was different. Eyes connected, Cassie couldn't have looked away even if she'd wanted to. When the climax broke over her she didn't even care that Ares would see the moisture in her eyes, she couldn't stop it.

He chased his own completion, his body jerking against hers, and she lamented the barrier stopping his seed from spilling into her. She felt it on a very primal level, that she was meant to be with this man. In every way. But she bit into his shoulder to stop herself from saying the words that wouldn't be welcome.

And yet, as she gripped him close to her, legs wrapped around his back, hearts slowing down in unison, she desperately tried to tell herself that it was just hormones and amazing sex, that she couldn't possibly have fallen for this haunted lone wolf.

But she knew she had and that this would be her cross to bear for ever. She wanted to hate him for that. But she couldn't even do that.

'Wear this.'

Cassie took the baseball cap Ares handed her, and put it on her head. She'd tied her hair back into a bun. They were in a chauffeur-driven SUV being taken from the airport to the museum. It felt strange to be back in a busy city again. Jarring.

She still felt a little over-sensitised after the plane. She'd noticed that, after making love, Ares had washed and dressed and left her to do the same, saying something about making calls.

Since they'd landed he'd been solicitous but was clearly drawing back. Putting boundaries back in place. Boundaries that had never really been there.

And it felt so wrong. Cassie wanted to stamp her foot and demand he look at her. She smiled at herself mockingly—exactly how a petulant princess would behave.

They pulled to a stop on the banks of the Arno river, in front of the imposing building that housed the famous galleries. It rose up, dominating the landscape. Cassie still couldn't quite believe Ares had thought of this.

He was out of the SUV now and holding open the door, looking around. She saw him nod to someone in dark nondescript clothing getting out of another vehicle and asked, 'Who is that?'

'Your security. They've been replaced by a new team, vetted by me.'

Feeling desperate at this evidence of her real world encroaching ever more steadily, she said, 'But you can protect me.'

He took her hand, and said, 'I'm not taking any chances.'

Cassie couldn't help her bruised heart from wishing he meant *not taking any chances* because he cared for her, but she knew he was just doing his job. Before they took a step towards the galleries he faced her and said, 'When we're finished here I'm going to hand you back over to your team and you are not to try to evade them again, understand me?'

He sounded so stern that Cassie looked at him and said meekly, 'Yes.'

Still holding her hand, he led her into the main gallery. Ares had organised the tickets ahead of time and so they were able to join the throngs of other tourists, all drinking in the spectacular art. But already Cassie knew she'd have to come again because this trip was ruined by the distraction of knowing that these were her last few moments with Ares.

So, greedily, she clung to his hand. Not that he was pulling away. And she revelled in standing close to him. Smelling him guiltily like someone with a scent kink, rather than taking in the spine-tingling beauty of Botticelli's *The Birth of Venus*.

As they moved from one gallery to the next Cassie asked him, 'Where will you go from here? Back to New York?'

A muscle ticced in his jaw. 'No, not straight away. I'll go to London. I have some meetings lined up there.'

She squeezed his hand. 'I think you should contact your brother and sisters, Ares, let them in.'

He glanced down at her, a different man from the one who'd forced his way onto her boat. 'Like the way I let you in?'

But had he? Really? She forced a smile. 'Exactly, what could possibly go wrong?'

He looked a little arrested when she said that but then people jostled them from behind and his expression cleared and they continued moving with the flow of tourists.

After a while he said, 'I'll see.'

Cassie bumped him with her shoulder. 'No man is an island, Ares. Not even you, or my brother.'

She realised with a pang that they'd come full circle. They were back at the main entrance again. She wondered desperately if she could pretend that she hadn't noticed and go around the galleries again but Ares was saying, 'Your security team are waiting.'

She saw the sleek silver SUV and the guards. They looked stony. No doubt under orders not to mess up. Cassie felt sick. Nauseous. Desperate. She couldn't walk away from Ares without telling him…

She tightened her grip on his hand and looked up at him. 'Ares.'

Ares steeled himself and looked down. Cassie's upturned face was visible from under the lip of the hat and he felt as though he knew every curve and dip and line as well as his own. Better.

'Cass, you need to go—'

She shook her head. 'No, I need to say something first.' She looked effortlessly regal in that moment, even in her trousers and silk T-shirt and flat shoes, designed to blend in with the crowd. Her cross-body bag. Who'd he been kidding? She would never blend in. She was a queen.

Not his queen.

'Ares, do you really believe it's not possible to have more? Something real? Love?'

Ares's gut clenched hard. For the first time in his life it wasn't so easy to dismiss. Because something had changed in him. Some chink had opened up and illuminated a space for wanting something he'd never wanted before. And it was her fault. He hardened his heart. When had it become so damned soft?

The moment you saw her dancing in that bar, and you know it.

He shook his head. 'I'm sure it exists for some, maybe even for you, some day. But not for me.' His stubbornness was like a hard piece of granite inside him. And there was something else he was too cowardly to admit to. *Fear.*

Cassie glanced over at where her people were waiting and back to Ares, eyes wide and beseeching. 'You do know you deserve to be happy, Ares? These last few days…it's possible to have that. All the time.'

The notion that they could really have that glorious togetherness without the world getting in the way was so…huge that Ares shut it down. She was talking nonsense. It had just been a moment.

If she left now then she'd have a chance of retaining that bright nature, but if Ares did what his dark soul really wanted to do, which was to spirit her away and keep her for himself, then he *would* dim that light for ever. He couldn't give her what she wanted. *Deserved.*

Something had been irreparably broken in him when he'd been so traumatised at a young age. He'd lost a sense of childish optimisim and innocence. He'd cut himself off to protect himself and it was too late to change that now.

'Ares, I love you.'

She spoke the words and it was too late to demand she take them back. They existed. The chink was cracking open and Ares's very foundations were crumbling to pieces. *No.* She didn't mean it. He was not lovable. He would ruin her. A self-preserving protective reflex snapped into action.

'No,' he said fiercely. 'You don't. You think you do. It's been intense, that's all. You'll meet someone far better than me, Cass. Someone worthy of being your king.'

'*You* are worthy, Ares Drakos. I don't want anyone else. I won't. Will you?'

Ares looked at her and pushed down the ache in his chest and forced ice into his veins as he said as coolly as he could, 'Of course I will. Nothing lasts for ever.'

It doesn't, he told himself even more fiercely even as he felt as if a part of himself was dying inside. He still wanted her, that was all. It would fade.

He saw the way she went pale and a light went out of her eyes. He told himself it was a good thing, because she would get over this and him. He needed her to hate him a little. So she would go and get on with her life and not look back. She was a queen. He had no claim to her.

'You need to go, princess. They're waiting.' He needed her to go. Now. Because the longer she stood there looking stricken, the more conflicted he felt.

But then he saw the way her eyes flashed at his use of *princess* and some colour came back into her cheeks. She took a step back and he saw her security team looking around, making ready.

'No doubt you're right, nothing lasts for ever.' She smiled but it was brittle. 'I'm just not as experienced in these matters as you. Goodbye, Ares.'

Oof. Ares felt the words like a blow. He deserved that. He'd made her hate him. Good. She turned and was walking away, through the crowds to the discreet SUV parked at the kerb. And then she was getting inside and the door was closing and the security guy jumped into the front and the car was pulling away and disappearing into the traffic. And just like that... she was gone and at that moment the sun went behind a massive cloud.

London, two days later

Ares was watching the news, specifically a report from Sadat Sur Mer about Crown Princess Cassandra and how she'd appeared in public for the first time in days to allay the rumours and speculation that all was not well in the palace of Mansur de Roche.

She was greeting a crowd, wearing a simple but smart blue dress, colour-toned to match her shoes. Hair up and sleek. Oozing regal elegance. It made him think of her in that white silk dress she'd worn for dinner, in Spetses. How she'd said, *'I'll never get to wear a dress like this at home.'*

She was bending down now to greet a little girl who was shy. Cassie's smile was so infectious that the little girl reached out to touch Cassie's cheek and

Cassie took her hand and spoke to her, making the girl giggle.

Ares didn't even realise he'd put a hand to his chest to alleviate an ache. She would be an amazing mother. And queen. The people clearly adored her.

'Ares... *Ares...?*'

Scowling at the interruption, Ares turned to find his assistant in the doorway. She looked at her watch. 'Your flight to New York is ready and waiting at the airfield. The driver is downstairs.'

It was time to move on.

Sadat Sur Mer, The Palace

Cassie opened the button at the top of the blue dress she'd worn for the walkabout. She felt constricted. She wanted to strip naked and dive into cool blue waters. Already, it felt like a dream—her Greek odyssey—and she hated that it was fading.

At night she dreamt of it though, and him, and it was clear and vivid. She'd woken with tears on her cheeks this morning. Pathetic.

There was a knock on her office door and she scooped Zoe up into her arms. The dog licked Cassie's face just as Pierre walked in and he couldn't hide his delicate shudder of disapproval.

He had a file under his arm, and Cassie already knew what it was. The dreaded prospective husbands.

'If these are the same as when I left I'm not interested. None of them were suitable.'

Pierre stopped in his tracks. Cassie knew she was

different since she'd come back. Less meek and unsure. Less amenable. But in a fair and firm way. Less smiley. Pierre said, 'No, these are new candidates.' He sent her a glance, not sure how to deal with this version of the crown princess.

Cassie sat down and said, 'You can leave it there. I'll have a look later.'

'But—'

She looked at Pierre and he stopped talking. 'Thank you.'

He cleared his throat. 'There's just one more thing, Your Highness.'

'Yes?'

'The pre-coronation ball.'

'Yes?' The ball would be held the night before the coronation, and would be a chance to welcome all of the VIP guests who'd been invited from all over the world. It would be Cassie's first properly formal event as almost queen. Her last as a crown princess. The eyes of the world would be on her. She instinctively covered her inner wrist where she'd had the tattoo done. So far she'd manaaged to keep it hidden from view. But Ares had been right, someone would inevitably notice it and her twin sister would no longer belong just to her.

Pierre was saying now, 'We feel that the ball would be a good opportunity to also invite any possible future consorts…so if you should find someone suitable among the new suggestions, let me know and we'll invite them.'

Cassie's insides roiled nauseously at the thought of even looking at another man. She swallowed it down. She was a queen. She didn't get to have much of a choice in this matter. 'Fine, thank you, Pierre.'

When Pierre had left, Cassie put Zoe down on the floor and opened up the folder. This was her life now, she had to suck it up.

Much to her dismay, when she looked at the candidates there were at least three who she couldn't find any reason not to consider. One of these men might one day soon become her husband. She battled the resurgence of the nausea and picked up the phone, saying to Pierre, 'I have the names of three of the candidates. Are you ready?'

Pierre tripped over his words, he was so obviously ecstatic. 'Yes, yes, please, Your Highness, I'm ready.'

She rattled off the names and put the phone down. There. Her fate was now all but sealed. Within two weeks she'd be Queen of Sadat and there would be a marriage announcement.

As much as Cassie was genuinely looking forward to taking her place among the kings and queens of Sadat on her coronation day, she felt acutely lonely at the thought of doing it alone.

Even though Caius would be there, at least. The public appeared to be ready to forgive his lack of royal bloodline. And he would know what she was going through.

But the one person who she would really want to see there wouldn't be anywhere near Sadat. Ares. She hated him all over again in that moment for making her fall for him. For making her wish for his solid presence. For his beautiful body. The way he made her feel. The way he saw her.

But of course she didn't hate him at all. She loved him. The bastard.

CHAPTER TWELVE

Ten days later...

THE STREETS OF New York were too busy. Loud. Jarring. Ares had done his best to re-acclimatise since his return but the place he'd called home for years now felt like an alien planet.

Had it always been so grimy? So grey? So...closed in with tall buildings? Everyone seemed so much in a rush. So desperate. No one smiled.

A few days before when Ares had been leaving his office building after his final meeting, he'd smiled at his security guy. Who hadn't smiled back. Ares had realised he was smiling like a loon, in some attempt to be polite, or *nice*, and the man had been frowning at him as if he had two heads. 'You OK, Mr Drakos?'

Ares had promptly broken out in a cold sweat. What the hell was wrong with him? Smiling at people and expecting the same in return? He was in a city where that could be considered slightly homicidal behaviour. He'd once been a fully signed up member of the make-no-eye-contact, unsmiling public.

Before he'd met *her*. So now he was scowling as he

pushed open the doors to his offices. He'd just taken a meeting with a new client in a hotel downtown and had walked all the way back, feeling too restless to sit in a car or take the subway.

He barely noticed the same security guard behind the desk, too busy fighting off memories and images.

He kept seeing Cassie disappear into the back of the SUV, the door closing behind her. The reality that he would never see her again, except on a TV screen or perhaps somehow through Caius, was like a burr under his skin. He'd had a dream the night before, of watching her get married to some faceless chinless prince. Beaming at him. Confetti. Kissing him.

Ares had woken in a sweat, heart pounding. He did smile now as the elevator carried him up to the penthouse office but it was grim. It was small comfort that nightmares of boats had been replaced with nightmares of Cassie with another man.

He got to his office—empty because his staff had long finished for the day. It was late. But he was still too restless to go back to his empty apartment nearby. It was on evenings like this he would have sought out the company of someone like Caius, but Caius was in Sadat, because the coronation was happening any day now.

Everything seemed to circle back to Cassie.

He could call up a woman. Sex. Surely that would alleviate this building sense of panic?

But the thought of a woman who wasn't Cassie... made his insides churn. Irritated with himself and his inability to just…settle back into his life, Ares poured himself a slug of whiskey and turned on the TV.

A news channel came on and as if the universe was intent on punishing him, or torturing him, it showed images of Sadat Sur Mer and the reporter was gushing about the excitement of the upcoming coronation as images of Cassie proliferated in the background.

Cassie as a baby, then as a small cherubic child, and a slightly gawky teenager with braces and now… His heart ached. As a beautiful young woman ready to step into her own power. And what power that was. She was magnificent.

Then an image of a man came on the screen. Some blond pretty man. With a toothy smile. Ares turned up the volume as the reporter said breathlessly, 'Prince Stefan has been invited to the pre-coronation ball tomorrow night. It's widely rumoured that after the coronation there will be an announcement of nuptials…'

Ares muted the sound, unable to listen to any more. He could see that man and Cassie together. They'd make a photogenic couple. They'd have even more photogenic kids. Royal kids.

Something hot roared to life inside Ares, deep down, rising up. Jealousy. No. More than jealousy. *She was his.* Not that insipid man's. She'd told him she loved him.

Desperation replaced the panic. He couldn't let this just…happen. He needed to see her. Look in her eyes. See the moment when she'd show regret for what she'd said because she couldn't have possibly meant it. And then maybe he could walk away and feel some peace.

Well, not peace, he'd never feel that again, but some measure of being able to get on with his life. If he knew for sure that she didn't want him.

Ares's heart pounded at the thought that he might look into her eyes and see something else entirely.

He should leave her be. But it was too late. She'd melted something inside him. Rewired him. Made him want…connection. A chance to strive for another kind of existence. Happiness. *Love*. He knew he loved her. He'd known it as soon as her happiness had become paramount to him.

Before he could overthink it, Ares dug out his phone and dialled his assistant, issuing instructions. After a few minutes his assistant said, 'Sorry, boss, it looks like tomorrow is the earliest I can get you out of here.'

Ares cursed. It would have to do. 'Book it.' On his way back out of his office building Ares stopped in his tracks by the security guard's desk. The man looked up. Ares said, 'You know, it wouldn't kill you to smile once in a while.' And then he walked out. Smiling.

Cassie's face hurt from smiling so much. She'd never felt less like smiling in her life. And her hand ached from greeting all of the dignitaries. And her feet ached in the high heels.

She was in full crown princess uniform in her midnight-blue silk dress with voluminous silk skirts overlaid with tulle. The strapless bodice was boned, tucking her in and allowing only an acceptable amount of cleavage. Family heirloom jewels, sapphires and diamonds, glinted at her ears, neck and wrist.

She wore a white sash across her dress, adorned with ceremonial ribbons and brooches to signify her country's glorious military history and its independence.

Her hair was up and teased into a complicated chignon and she wore a diamond tiara that was weighing heavier and heavier on her head.

Unfortunately Caius hadn't been able to help her with this. He was somewhere in the background, easing himself back into acceptability. At least he was here, even if not by her side. It had been good to see him again.

She was firmly shutting out the face of the one person she *really* would like to see but the prospect of him appearing in the endless line-up bowing before her was about as likely as a unicorn materialising.

Her insides tensed as she recognised the next person. Crown Prince Stefan de Wilhelm of Danzerra, a small monarchy in central Europe. A prime candidate to be her husband. She sensed the hush that went up around them as everyone watched to see them meet for the first time.

He bowed before her and Cassie noticed a bald patch on the top of his head. She had the bizarre urge to giggle and she knew it was hysteria. He straightened and smiled. She felt sorry for her unkind observation. He was a perfectly handsome and potentially good candidate for marriage.

She let him take her hand. 'Thank you so much for coming, Prince—'

Suddenly there was a commotion near them and Cassie looked away from the prince to see a tall man bearing down on them, with a visibly distressed Pierre running to catch up and several of her security guards.

Ares. *No.* She had to be dreaming. Hallucinating, Brought on by the exhaustion of this interminable line-up. She blinked. But when she opened her eyes again Ares Drakos was now standing beside the prince.

Cassie was struck by the almost comical disparity in *everything*. Their size, looks, charisma. And then she realised…this wasn't a dream. Ares Drakos was really standing here, in… She looked him up and down. In worn jeans and a loose shirt. Hair wild. Was his beard bigger? He looked deliciously scruffy and achingly sexy and thoroughly out of place. And yet so *perfect*.

Pierre pushed forward, sweating. 'I'm so sorry, Your Highness, this man somehow managed to get through the security cordon—we'll have him removed—'

But then another voice joined in. 'Ares? What the hell are you doing here?'

It was Caius. But neither Cassie nor Ares looked away from each other. She just asked, 'What *are* you doing here?'

She was in shock. Numb. But she could feel sensation returning and it was like when the numbness of icy cold retreated and the heat returned painfully. She realised she'd been cold since she'd walked away from him. After baring her heart to him. After his rejection.

She strove to not let herself melt. This could mean nothing at all. She hated him. *She loved him.*

'Ares?' The silence was so profound around them but Cassie barely noticed.

'I needed to see you. To look you in the eye when I asked you...'

'Asked me what?'

'If you really meant it. What you said in Florence?'

Cassie felt something bloom inside her. Hope. She arched a brow. 'You mean when I said I loved you?'

A gasp went up around them.

Ares said, 'Yes, when you said you loved me. Did you mean it?'

How could he not see it shining out of her like a bright light? She nodded. 'Yes, I meant it. I love you, Ares.'

He stepped forward and put his hands around her face, tipping it up. Cassie felt the tiara slide a little precariously and grinned. He was unravelling her already and she couldn't care less.

'I love you, Cassie, but I felt selfish. How can I ask you to be mine when you need someone who'll be so much more suited?'

Cassie put her hands on Ares's, sliding her fingers between his. 'I don't need some prince.'

Neither of them noticed the splutter of indignation coming from the prince who was still standing there.

Cassie continued, 'I need *you*. But I know it's a lot to ask. You'd be giving up a lot...for me.'

Ares shook his head, fervent. 'I would give up my life for you.'

There was a distinct sigh from the crowd.

Ares went on, 'My life means nothing without you. I want it all, Cassie. I want to give you everything you've ever dreamed of and I want to be happy. You've shown me that it's possible. With you, I know I can do anything.'

'We'd have to have children...if we can. They'll bear my name.'

Ares's eyes gleamed. 'They'll have the bravest and most magnificent mother in the world, why wouldn't they bear your name?'

He said, 'I'm sorry that it took me a few days to figure this out. I fell for you the moment I saw you in that bar, determined to have an experience.'

Cassie blushed. 'I adore you, Ares. You see me. I've never really had that, except for Caius and he doesn't really count.'

There was another splutter of indignation from Caius's direction but Cassie went on, 'I can't take on this role without a real partner. I'd hoped for respect and companionship but after meeting you... I want so much more. The thought of becoming queen and settling for someone else...has nearly killed me.'

Ares's eyes looked suspiciously bright. 'I'm so sorry I let you go, Cass.'

He gathered her to him and kissed her, deep and thoroughly. When he pulled back she said breathlessly, 'Don't be sorry... I don't think either of us were expecting this...'

They looked at each other dreamily for a long moment, until Caius's voice broke the intense silence. 'Will someone please tell me what the hell is going on?'

Ares took Cassie's hand in his. She was beaming. Sore facial muscles forgotten. Tiara askew. She tore her gaze from Ares's and looked around. The great and good of the world staring at them. The prince's mouth was gaping open like a stunned fish. Pierre looked as if he was on the verge of a heart attack. And her brother was murderous. She'd never been happier.

Ares said, 'Can we go somewhere private?'

She looked back at him and her insides liquefied with desire. She nodded. But then she winced when she took a step and her feet protested in the new shoes.

Ares was immediately concerned. 'What is it?'

'Sore feet.'

Within two seconds he'd swept her up into his arms. One of her shoes fell to the floor. Ares looked at Caius and said, 'I know you want to break every bone in my body but the fact is that I love your sister and I'm going to go somewhere now to ask her if she'll marry me. If that's OK with you?'

Caius looked as if he were about to explode but then he looked at Cassie and he must have seen her incandescent happiness because after a long moment his features softened. He said, 'Aw, hell. Go. Not with my blessing, it's too soon for that. But just go.'

As Ares swept Cassie out of the ornate ballroom and away from the hundreds of guests she could have sworn she heard Pierre ask Caius, 'Is there any chance he's related to the Greek royal family at all? Any royal family?'

In the end it didn't matter that Ares was not related to any royal family. Their moment had gone viral around the world and everyone had fallen in love with Ares and Cassie and their love story.

Pierre hadn't had a hope of standing in their way. Neither had Caius, who eventually did come to terms with his best friend becoming his brother-in-law.

Cassie had been crowned queen, with Ares close by her side at all times. Soon afterwards their engagement had been announced by the palace to no one's surprise.

EPILOGUE

Five years later—Sadat Sur Mer, The Palace

Cassie had worked hard to dissolve a lot of the old structures standing between the royal family and the people of Sadat and now the palace was regularly humming with community activities, visiting tourists, and the family were involved in day-to-day life in a way that no other royal family had ever been.

But here in this wing, their private wing, there were no intrusions. Cassie walked from her office across the hall to where Ares's office was. He'd moved Drakos Security to Sadat over the past few years and it had now become a hub for the latest security technology and best defence systems in the world.

His new office building was in the centre of the town, an architecturally cutting-edge structure, but Ares liked to use his office at the palace because his main priority was as the king consort. And husband. And now, father.

Cassie stopped in the doorway and chuckled at the sight. Ares was lying back on a soft couch, with two smaller bodies sprawled on top of him, all of them snoring gently. A book was strewn to the side.

They'd had twins three years ago. Isabella and Calliope. Bella and Calli. Bella was the firstborn, and a reference to Belle, Cassie's beloved lost sister. They were identical twins, taking after both parents. They had blonde hair but Cassie could see it was already turning darker, and they had the dark eyes of their father.

She put a hand to her distended belly. Their little boy was due in a couple of months. The girls' suggestions for names so far had ranged from Calli's favourite thing in the world—Unicorn! To Bella's suggestion—Baby Brotha!

Since the arrival of the children, Ares had reached out to his own siblings and they'd finally connected. It had been a happy reunion. It had been easier with his sisters, but Ares had also met his brother, Axel, and was making plans to work with him, providing security for Drakos Shipping, and so he was returning to the fold on his terms.

As often as they could, Cassie and Ares went back to the villa on Spetses and revelled in a few days of isolation and freedom. Sometimes alone when they could manage it, sometimes with the girls.

They updated their wish lists all the time and Ares was extremely assiduous in making sure they ticked off all the items. On their honeymoon to the south of Spain, Ares had taken Cassie horse-riding on Adalucian horses on the beach at dawn.

Motorcycling along Route 66 still had to be done but Cassie was sure they'd get around to it, some day.

Caius had gone on his own journey to find happiness but that was not Cassie's story to tell.

Much later, when the girls had been put to bed and their nanny was on the night shift, Cassie moved against Ares. His heat and strength and love surrounded her as they moved together in a dance as old as time.

His hand was splayed on her belly and another hand cupped her breast as he took her from behind, thrusting deep inside and taking them both on a languorous sensual dance.

He put his mouth close to her ear. 'Remind me when we have to stop having sex?'

Cassie huffed a laugh. 'Never…never stop.'

And then she cried out as her climax broke over her, and Ares gripped her tight as he followed her. They lay in sated bliss for long moments and then Ares pulled the sheet up and curled himself around Cassie's body, arms stretching around her, to her belly, a hand over their son.

'Thank you,' he said into her ear, sleepily.

Cassie smiled and lifted his hand, pressing a kiss to it. 'Thank *you*, for coming back to me.'

'Always and for ever,' promised Ares.

* * * * *

*Did you fall in love with
Bodyguard's Royal Temptation?
Then make sure to check out the next instalment in
the Royal House of Sadat duet, coming soon!
In the meantime, explore these other
stories by Abby Green!*

The Heir Dilemma
On His Bride's Terms
Rush to the Altar
Billion-Dollar Baby Shock
Bride of Betrayal

Available now!

Get up to 4 Free Books!

We'll send you 2 free books from each series you try PLUS a free Mystery Gift.

Both the **Harlequin Presents** and **Harlequin Medical Romance** series feature exciting stories of passion and drama.

YES! Please send me 2 FREE novels from Harlequin Presents or Harlequin Medical Romance and my FREE gift (gift is worth about $10 retail). After receiving them, if I don't wish to receive any more books, I can return the shipping statement marked "cancel." If I don't cancel, I will receive 6 brand-new larger-print novels every month and be billed just $7.19 each in the U.S., or $7.99 each in Canada, or 4 brand-new Harlequin Medical Romance Larger-Print books every month and be billed just $7.19 each in the U.S. or $7.99 each in Canada, a savings of 20% off the cover price. It's quite a bargain! Shipping and handling is just 50¢ per book in the U.S. and $1.25 per book in Canada.* I understand that accepting the 2 free books and gift places me under no obligation to buy anything. I can always return a shipment and cancel at any time. The free books and gift are mine to keep no matter what I decide.

Choose one:
☐ **Harlequin Presents Larger-Print** (176/376 BPA G36Y)
☐ **Harlequin Medical Romance** (171/371 BPA G36Y)
☐ **Or Try Both!** (176/376 & 171/371 BPA G36Z)

Name (please print)

Address   Apt. #

City   State/Province   Zip/Postal Code

Email: Please check this box ☐ if you would like to receive newsletters and promotional emails from Harlequin Enterprises ULC and its affiliates. You can unsubscribe anytime.

Mail to the Harlequin Reader Service:
IN U.S.A.: P.O. Box 1341, Buffalo, NY 14240-8531
IN CANADA: P.O. Box 603, Fort Erie, Ontario L2A 5X3

Want to explore our other series or interested in ebooks? **Visit www.ReaderService.com or call 1-800-873-8635.**

---

*Terms and prices subject to change without notice. Prices do not include sales taxes, which will be charged (if applicable) based on your state or country of residence. Canadian residents will be charged applicable taxes. Offer not valid in Quebec. This offer is limited to one order per household. Books received may not be as shown. Not valid for current subscribers to the Harlequin Presents or Harlequin Medical Romance series. All orders subject to approval. Credit or debit balances in a customer's account(s) may be offset by any other outstanding balance owed by or to the customer. Please allow 4 to 6 weeks for delivery. Offer available while quantities last.

Your Privacy—Your information is being collected by Harlequin Enterprises ULC, operating as Harlequin Reader Service. For a complete summary of the information we collect, how we use this information and to whom it is disclosed, please visit our privacy notice located at https://corporate.harlequin.com/privacy-notice. Notice to California Residents – Under California law, you have specific rights to control and access your data. For more information on these rights and how to exercise them, visit https://corporate.harlequin.com/california-privacy. For additional information for residents of other U.S. states that provide their residents with certain rights with respect to personal data, visit https://corporate.harlequin.com/other-state-residents-privacy-rights/.